MY GREAT SUCCESS AND OTHER FAILURES

CATHERINE WILKINS

nosy crow

For Margaret, Eileen and Sheila, my brilliant aunties.

C. W.

First published in the UK in 2015 by Nosy Crow Ltd
This edition published in 2019 by Nosy Crow Ltd
The Crow's Nest, 14 Baden Place, Crosby Row
London SE1 1YW, UK

Nosy Crow and associated logos are trademarks and/or registered
trademarks of Nosy Crow Ltd

Text © Catherine Wilkins, 2015
Cover illustration © Joel Holland, 2019
Interior illustrations © Sarah Horne, 2015

The right of Catherine Wilkins to be identified as the author of this work
has been asserted by her in accordance with the Copyright, Designs
and Patents Act 1988.

A CIP catalogue record for this book is available from the British Library

Printed and bound in Great Britain by Clays Ltd, Elcograf S.p.A.
Typeset by Tiger Media

Papers used by Nosy Crow are made from wood grown in
sustainable forests.

ISBN: 978 0 85763 490 0

www.nosycrow.com

CHAPTER 1

"Jessica!" my mum hollers up the stairs. "Can you come down here, please?"

"I'm busy!" I holler back, still engrossed in the cartoon I'm drawing in which my school gets taken over by aliens. (The next issue of our comic is about The Future.)

"Did you hear me?" my mum shouts back. "Come down!"

"I can't!" I yell. "I'm right in the middle of something."

"Come down here this minute! I want to talk to

you and I'm not going to do it shouting up the stairs!"

Well then, why doesn't *she* come up here to talk to *me*? That seems like it would be the polite thing to do. I put down my pencil. This is just *typical*. Adults today are so impatient. I think it must be all the caffeine in their diets.

TYPICAL

I thump irritably down the stairs and sigh lavishly at the bottom, where my mum greets me holding my school report. "What?"

"Well, you can drop the attitude for starters," Mum tells me, seemingly displeased, which is odd, because I think what she meant to say was, "Thank you for abandoning your important work and coming all the way downstairs on a merest whim."

"Jessica, we'd like to talk to you about your school report." Dad comes and stands next to Mum, and then they usher me into the living room like it's their office or something and I am about to be fired from work.

"O-K," I reply, sitting on the sofa nonplussed.

I wonder if everyone gets this treatment from their parents. I wonder if Joshua, Tanya, Amelia and my best friend, Natalie, are sitting on sofas all around our town about to be lectured.

Well, Amelia probably won't be because she is more or less top of the class in everything. And Natalie is pretty good, too. My friends Emily, Megan and Fatimah tend to be worse than me because they like to mess around, but I get the impression their parents are as fun-loving and laid-back as they are, so they probably won't be in trouble or anything.

I bet I'm the only one unlucky enough to be stuck in the middle of a Venn diagram made up of "overambitious parents" and "not quite good enough grades". It's not fair. I mean, where's the *humanity*?

My little brother, Ryan, is sitting on the floor next to Lady, our new rescue dog, pushing a truck backwards and forwards. Unusually for him, he's not doing the sound effects at the same time so it's actually quiet for once. My older sister, Tammy (who doesn't live here), is cheekily using the family Internet at the kitchen table.

"Well," begins my dad, "your report is a bit mixed this term."

3

"Cool." I decide to attempt a joke. "Variety is the spice of life and all that."

"No," says Mum. "It's not good enough. You're not using your full potential. Listen to this: *History – Jessica behaves well in class and generally pays attention, but her written work often includes more drawings than is strictly necessary.*"

"That sounds like a compliment to me," I say.

Mum continues: "*Geography – Jessica drew a beautiful illustration of the effects of erosion, but then failed to complete the rest of the questions. Perhaps she should spend more time writing and less time drawing.* What do you say to that?" she finishes.

"Well, I don't really like geography," I explain. "But the – quote – 'beautiful' picture I drew showed I understood it all. So where's the harm?"

Mum sighs sadly. "Jessica, you're eleven, and that's too old to keep turning everything into a picture. It's not like you're Ryan's age any more."

"Hey." Ryan looks up, but he hasn't really been listening. I know I'm not six any more, for crying out loud. I'm *much* better at drawing now than when I was six.

"You need to scale back on the cartoons and put

more effort into writing," says Mum, looking at Dad to back her up. "Doesn't she?" she prompts menacingly.

"Yes," Dad agrees quickly.

"You'll be at secondary school soon," adds Mum. "They won't stand for it there."

"Read what my art teacher, Mrs Cooper, says about me," I request.

"Well, obviously *she* loves you. And we're not saying you're not talented," says Mum.

"Read it," I insist.

Mum starts reluctantly. "*Jessica is a fantastic and enthusiastic student who embraces every new challenge inventively. She has a fine eye for detail and her work on the set design for the school musical was outstanding. Jessica will benefit from the resources and opportunities of a much bigger art department at secondary school, as there is not much more we can teach her here!*

"Yes, well, that's all very good," admits Mum, "but don't go thinking that means you don't need to put any effort into other subjects."

"Aren't you proud of me about my art stuff?" I ask.

"Oh yes, *very* proud," enthuses Dad.

Mum shoots him a look that evidently makes him uncomfortable because he adds, "But everything in its place. Keep art in art lessons. Do proper work in proper subjects."

"Art *is* a proper subject," I protest. "It's one of the things that separates *Homo sapiens* from the Neanderthals."

This momentarily stumps my parents and they blink at me. "Well, that's as may be," says Mum finally.

"It's not like you're not bright," says Dad.

"That's great you know about Neanderthals and *Homo sapiens*," adds Mum. "This is why we're nagging you. It's important you let this great intelligence of yours show in your written school work."

"That's all we ask," chips in Dad.

"Because, ultimately, that's what's going to decide your future and help you get a job," says Mum. "You're never going to get an important job from drawing cartoons."

"Jess!" My sister, Tammy, charges into the living room. "I've got an important job for you. I need you to draw me a cartoon."

I hope I'm not the kind of person who would overuse the word "priceless" but that was *priceless*. Mum and Dad's faces: priceless.

I still can't work out if Tammy *PRICELESS* was listening to the conversation and did that on purpose, but the result was the same – priceless. I might stop using that word now. Ah, once more. *Priceless*.

AWKWARD Needless to say, dinner is awkward. Mum keeps shooting Tammy evils. Which is a shame, because the food is actually very nice today. It's macaroni cheese and salad, made from *supermarket-brand* ingredients, not *Super Saver Value* ones. (Goodbye, *economy drive*! You are gone but not forgotten.)

"Sit up straight, please, Ryan!" Mum is taking out her irritation on my little brother.

Ryan instantly strains his head up and makes himself stiff, as if he's playing musical statues. "Like this, Mummy?"

"Well, just sit sensibly," amends my dad.

Ryan exhales and flumps forward.

"Phew," he mutters, and eats more macaroni cheese.

"Oh, Tammy," says Mum, "while I remember, please stop changing the Google logo so much. I like the original."

"What?" says Tammy, bemused.

"I mean it," says Mum warningly. "I don't mind you using our Internet, but stop messing with it."

"Mum, that Google logo just changes by itself, depending on what day it is," I say. "Tammy's not doing it."

"What?" says Mum, looking confused and a bit annoyed.

"Sorry, because I know it's fun to blame me for everything," says Tammy. "By the way," she adds, "I think there's actually a meme of 'stupid things mums say', and that's one of the things on it."

"What's a meme?" asks Mum, getting ready to be really annoyed.

"It doesn't matter what a meme is," interrupts my dad. "Can we all please just have a nice meal?"

"Fine," says my mum sulkily. "Jessica, sit up properly, please."

"OK. So it's for this protest," explains Tammy later in my room. "Well, it's more of a campaign, really. I think a punchy cartoon could really help spread the message and make people aware of the cause."

"What's the cause?" I ask.

"Climate change," says my sister. "People and corporations just aren't getting the message that they need to reduce their carbon footprints. The way we use energy is so damaging. We *have* to act now.

The planet is going to flood and we're probably the last generation that can do anything about it."

"Well, that sounds very serious," I say.

"It *is* serious," agrees Tammy. Then, clocking my face, "Is that a problem?"

"Well, my cartoons are usually, um ... *funny*," I say. (I don't mean to blow my own trumpet, but most of 6C agree.) "I'm not sure I could be funny about a serious subject like that. Wouldn't it be ... sort of ... inappropriate?"

"That's your *challenge*." Tammy looks disappointed in me. "This is the whole *point* of satire," she sighs.

"It is?"

"Of course. You take a serious subject that people avoid because it scares them – and you find a clever way to make them think about it in a new light. Then bingo – the comedy draws them in, and before they know it, they're engaged in being proper citizens."

OK. I have to admit, I didn't completely follow all of that. Though it *sounded* like it made sense. But I'm still not sure I've adequately expressed my concerns. "It's just—"

"Look, Jess," Tammy interrupts. "If you're not up to the job, that's fine. But you should know, if you're not part of the solution, you're part of the problem."

Not up to the job? How dare— *Do you know who I am?* I'm a brilliant cartoonist. My idol is Matt Groening. I want to be him or some kind of artist when I grow up. I am up to *every* job. Ever. (Every cartooning job, that is.)

"Of course I'm up to the job!" I splutter, trying not to sound too outraged.

"Great." Tammy grins and shakes my hand. "Welcome aboard."

CHAPTER 2

OK, so you know when I said I was up to the job? Well, I'm not so sure I'm up to the job. What was I *thinking*? Jobs are *hard*. Especially when you only understand half of what you've agreed to.

As I ride the bus to school the next day, I can't help but wonder if I've (in my dad's words) bitten off more than I can chew. (Admittedly he was saying it about when Lady picked up a really massive stick and couldn't fit through the park gate with it, but I'm pretty sure it works as a metaphor as well.)

I sat at my desk last night, trying to think of something funny about floods, but I couldn't really come up with anything. Well, unless the flood washed away our next-door neighbours, the VanDerks (very snooty, judgmental people who my parents are weirdly competitive with. Their daughter, Harriet, is in my year, and tried to make my life very difficult recently when I was set designing for the school musical).

Anyway, I'm pretty sure the idea of them being washed away in a flood is funny only to me. Well, and possibly Ryan and Tammy, but either way it's too niche a joke. Also, it would technically be *pro-*climate change, not anti. I sigh as I climb off the bus and head towards school.

Then I remember that there's a comic meeting today at lunch when I can show the others my brilliant Alien Future cartoon, and I start to perk up.

Things get even better when Nat sees me and cries enthusiastically, "Oh my God, Jess, you're just in time!" (I think that's quite a nice greeting.)

"What's up?" I say, coming over to the desks where Natalie (my best friend since our hokey-cokey days) and Amelia, my ex-frenemy™ (and now normal friend) sit.

"So, we're working on the school yearbook," explains Nat, "and we need to come up with some funny bits to describe people, like 'most likely to become a millionaire' but sillier, and I thought, you know, you're funny; you can help us come up with some stuff."

"Sure," I say, smiling. See, I *do* have **SKILZ** skilz. They *are* useful. (Ha. In your *face*, Mum and Dad.) "For the millionaire one, I nominate Tanya Harris." (And I'm not just saying that because she works on the comic with me, or because I'm still technically a bit scared of her. Plus, you know, I'm hardly even scared of her *at all* these days.)

Tanya "the Beef" Harris has gone from naughtiest girl in our year (and, really, the school) to best entrepreneur and business mogul. She's abandoned keying teachers' cars and tripping people in the corridor to become editor-in-chief of our comic, and she's in charge of distribution as well. I genuinely think she *could* become a millionaire in the future.

"Also, you still need to give us a cool photo and come up with your legacy thing," says Amelia.

It's still kind of weird that Amelia and I are friends now, when she used to bully me so much. She used to be very snide and undermining: wanting Natalie all to herself; always making passive-aggressive comments about my hair and insulting my intelligence.

But bizarrely, we really bonded when we worked on the set design of the school musical (partly united by how awful Harriet VanDerk was to us) and I finally saw Amelia's nice side. She *has* one! (I know, *right*?) And she even admitted bullying me, and apologised. But I still can't quite believe I have managed to be her friend. I must be pretty awesome and forgiving.

"Oh yeah, I'll bring in a photo. What pictures are you guys using?" I say.

"God, so many to choose from!" says Natalie.

"Look." She gets out her phone and starts flicking through loads of pictures of her dressed up as Dorothy in *The Wizard of Oz*, the school musical we just put on.

"I like that one." Amelia points at Nat's phone. "I've narrowed it down to these for me." Amelia then flicks through loads of pictures of her as Glinda the Good Witch. (Despite also doing set design, Amelia had a small part in the musical, because – let's face it – she is one of life's overachievers.)

"You guys have great photos," I tell them, starting to wonder what kind of photo I can use. I do have a photo of me standing proudly by a giant Yellow Brick Road backdrop we painted, but Amelia and Harriet are in that picture, too.

The thing is, I designed *most* of the sets, that's why Mrs Cooper, my art teacher, loves me so much at the moment. But I don't have a photo to *prove* it.

"Hey, gang," I say as I sit on one of the comfy chairs in the Quiet Reading Area outside the library. "I've drawn a great cartoon about our school in the future and—"

"Have you got a legacy thing?" interrupts Tanya. "For the yearbook?"

"Um, not yet, but—"

"Nah, me neither," she muses, looking uncharacteristically bothered.

"Well, if it's any consolation, I nominated you for 'most likely to become a millionaire'," I tell her.

Tanya immediately brightens. "Oh, that's brilliant! Thanks, Toons!"

(Tanya calls me Toons, because **TOONS!** I draw cartoons – geddit? Toons – *carTOONS*? Oh, why do I bother? Anyway. You can't groan or roll your eyes at me, because I didn't come up with it, Tanya did.)

"Ha," Joshua chuckles. "I would have nominated Lewis for that."

Joshua and Lewis make up the rest of the comic team. Joshua became my friend when I sort of fell out with Natalie earlier in Year Six. He plays basketball and thinks he's cool, but sort of is a *bit* cool. (But not as cool as he thinks he is.) He is funny, though. He played the Scarecrow in the school musical and I had no idea he could do physical comedy so well.

Lewis is still the person I know the least well out

of the three of them, despite being forced to work in close proximity with him when Tanya and Joshua were being diva-actor types and bunking off comic meetings. Lewis is shy and pedantic and obsessed with *Star Wars*. I suppose he could become a millionaire. Maybe.

"Well, I'm sure more than one person can be nominated for the millionaire prediction," I say kindly.

"Well, I wouldn't worry about that stuff anyway," Joshua says to Tanya. "We've got loads of achievements and stuff we can put for our legacies now. We both got outstanding mentions for *The Wizard*."

(Joshua has developed what I'm sure he imagines is the *cool* habit of abbreviating *The Wizard of Oz* to *The Wizard*. He says this instead of *the play* – which would actually be fewer syllables and therefore quicker if he's *that* worried about brevity.)

Anyway, he's right. They both got special mentions in assembly the other week. They were the comedy of the piece. Joshua was brilliant as the Scarecrow and

Tanya was hilarious as the Wicked Witch. I sort of do get why it went to their heads a bit. They worked really hard. (But so did I on set design.)

Tanya considers this. "Yeah, you're right. We've got *loads*, innit?"

"And loads of great photos," adds Joshua.

"Yeah!" enthuses Tanya.

"All right," I say, trying to sound jokily affronted. "You actor types don't have to rub it in our faces, just because you've got your legacies worked out."

"Oh, I've got mine too," pipes up Lewis.

"Lewis came top of computing," explains Joshua. Of course he did.

"Oh … cool, well done, Lewis!" I try and sound like I expected this on some level.

"Thanks," Lewis says flatly. I think his expression is somewhere between pity and disdain, but I'm not sure. I don't think he liked me lumping us together.

"Winners, innit, Toons?" says Tanya. "We're all winners!" (Is she including me in that?)

"Yes," I agree. "Well, now that that's all sorted, would anyone like to see my brilliant picture of our school being run by aliens in the future?" I sound slightly more annoyed than I'd meant to.

CHAPTER 3

"Jess, let's not go home, let's go to McDonald's and get milkshakes!" Nat and Amelia yank me off the bus, even though it's not my stop. They're still in high spirits from working on the yearbook, and the excitement of school nearly being over.

I text my mum I'll be late as we walk along. She'd be annoyed if I didn't. Ironically, she'd also be annoyed if she knew I was texting and walking at the same time, so I can't win.

I relax and put my phone back in my pocket. It's a nice sunny day and it's great to have fun with a happy Natalie and Amelia. It doesn't feel like that long ago they were banning me from their clandestine McDonald's trips. Oh well, water under the bridge.

It isn't until we join the queue that I remember I don't have any money. I mean, I *never* have any money, but it's only just started to become a bit of a problem. I didn't seem to need any before. Now that I hang out with Natalie and Amelia a bit more, it turns out that frequent milkshakes and sometimes chips require cash.

"I don't have any money," I tell Natalie, feeling awkward, even though this is almost part of a routine now.

"Don't worry, it's my turn to get Jessica's milkshake this time," says Amelia, opening her Hello Kitty purse. "Oh no," she says, examining its contents. "I don't have enough. Can you get it?" she asks Nat.

"I don't have enough either," says Natalie, counting the change in her hand. "Don't worry, Jess, just share mine."

Even though she's being really nice, I start to feel mortified. "It's fine, you guys. I'm really sorry

I never have any money. You don't have to get me anything."

Am I red? I feel like I'm going red. Stupid money. I feel angry that I don't have any, and angry that they dragged me in here without a thought for how embarrassed it makes me. I don't want to be a charity case. *Eurgh.* **EURGH**

"That's cool," says Amelia, apparently quite oblivious to any discomfort I'm in. "I would share with you too, but I'm funny about germs." Of course she is.

"It's fine. Honestly," I say. "Neither of you need to."

"Of course I'll share with you, Jess," says Nat. "You'd do the same for me, wouldn't you? If it was the other way round?"

"Yes," I say obligingly. Though actually, I like to think if it was the other way round, I'd be a bit more sensitive than her about it.

"Why should you suffer, just because your family are poor?" adds Amelia. And *a lot* more sensitive than Amelia is being.

"They're not, um, OK. It's fine. I'll find us a table," I mumble and exit this conversation.

It's too difficult to explain that, although my family went on an extended *economy drive* (Mum refused to buy anything except milk until everything in the cupboards was gone, including out-of-date kidney beans that were "probably fine"), and then we were *tightening our belts* (Mum refused to buy anything unless it was from the "reduced to clear" section or *Super Saver Value* brand), actually all that is over and we are back on regular *supermarket-brand crisps* and everything.

It's just that the possibility of a pocket-money rise is "non-negotiable" until we are more stable and back on our feet properly.

Nat and Amelia join me and I slurp some of Natalie's milkshake. On the plus side, it is nice and refreshing on this hot day. On the downside, they're still talking about blimmin' legacies.

"What do you think you'll choose, Jess?" asks Nat.

"Oh, um. Well, I guess cartoons is what I do mostly," I say. Natalie and Amelia exchange a slight look. "What?"

"We thought you might say something like that,"

says Amelia, kind of sadly.

"It's just" – Nat pauses, looking like she's trying to be tactful – "being good at cartoons isn't really a legacy thing," she explains kindly.

"Why not?" I say, surprised. "That's my thing."

"Well, it's not a *thing*," says Nat.

"It is too a *thing*," I counter childishly.

"Jess, and I say this with love, it's not a *proper thing*," says Nat patiently.

"Have you been talking to my parents?" I ask her.

"What? No." She sounds confused.

"Come on," I implore. "The cartoon I drew of our school as hell that went round everywhere? The comic I set up with Joshua and Tanya? It's famous in Year Six – people ask me to draw stuff on their rough books for them. I'm the cartoon person. It's in my nickname and everything."

"The thing is," tries Amelia, "that comic is with three other people. It's not just yours. And those three people all have other stuff going on as well."

"Yeah, they all have other stuff they're good at," agrees Natalie. (Is the implication that I *don't* have other stuff I'm good at? Oh God, *do* I not have other stuff I'm good at? *Have* I put all my eggs in one proverbial, if expertly drawn, basket? Are my parents *right*?)

"Think about it, anyway," says Amelia, taking another slurp of milkshake. I nod, reeling.

"Isn't this great?" says Nat happily, waving her hands expansively. "Smell that summer breeze." (The door bangs open and I can mainly smell petrol, but I think there's a summer breeze in there somewhere as well.) "And we've got our whole lives ahead of us!" she adds delightedly.

I smile politely, but my head is elsewhere. I'm not sure this *is* so great. For the first time I feel slightly worried about my future and concerned that I'm not actually equipped to deal with it.

I mean, it's one thing batting off my parents' concerns. But when their view is corroborated by my *peers*…? Well, you'd have to be mad not to pay it some attention. What's going on?

At home I head to the kitchen and find my sister, Tammy, arriving at the back door. "Don't worry, I

won't be here long," she tells my aggrieved-looking
mother. "I won't even stay for dinner."

"You won't want to, veg-head.
It's sausage and mash and it's
nearly ready," replies Mum
bluntly.

"Cup of tea?" Dad enters
the kitchen and puts the kettle
on. Mum nods gratefully.

Ryan skids into the kitchen on his knees and grabs
my dad's legs. "Gotcha!" he yells at Dad's trousers.
"Die, evil monster! Die!"

"You'll have to move, Ryan," says Dad. "I need to
use the kettle."

"Never!" cries Ryan. "And, Daddy? Don't,
whatever you do, tickle me."

Honestly, kids think they're so good at reverse
psychology, and they're so rubbish at it.

"Oh, I've no intention of tickling you," says Dad
matter-of-factly. "No intention whatso—" Suddenly
my dad lunges downwards and starts tickling Ryan,
who shrieks with delight and lets go of my dad's legs.
My dad escapes and gets cups out of the cupboard.

"Ryan, get up off the dirty floor," instructs Mum.

"Tammy, go home to your own house. We're busy. Jessica…" She pauses, possibly realising we haven't said hello yet. "Hello, poppet. How was school?"

"DADDDDEEEEEEEEE!" Ryan takes another lunge at Dad's legs.

"That's *enough* now, Ryan," says Dad in his stern voice, surprising Ryan into sitting up, disappointed. "I'm making hot drinks here; it's not safe. We'll play later."

Mildly pacified by the promise of "later", Ryan goes back into the living room to find Lady.

Tammy starts rooting through the cupboard."I just need to… By the way, why do you have so many plastic bags here? You should be using bags for life and reusing them."

"Excuse me," says Mum indignantly. "We do reuse them!"

Tammy takes out a grocery receipt from one of the bags. "Paper," she declares almost triumphantly. "You know how to tell whether you can recycle it or not, right? You have to – Hang on… Wow! Is this…?" Tammy holds up the receipt, seeming temporarily speechless. "This isn't from 1982, is it?" (*Very* temporarily.)

"No," sighs Mum. "Whatever the problem is, I'm sure we're very sorry, now can you please—"

Tammy pauses and looks awestruck at my mum. "Wait… How did you spend this *little* on a weekly food shop for a family of *four*?"

This receipt must be from either the economy drive or the belt-tightening extravaganza.

"Oh." Mum appears as blindsided by this question as Tammy was by the receipt discovery. "Well, I cook a lot of meals from scratch," says Mum, thinking, "and I shop carefully."

"Mum," says Tammy seriously, looking at Mum in wonder. "I never thought I would say this, but I need you to teach me how to cook."

Everyone stares at each other in shock.

CHAPTER 4

"But I thought food was 'just fuel', and cooking was a pretentious, bourgeois activity?" says Mum, partly enjoying this turnaround and still partly – I think – incredulous.

"Yeah, yeah," says Tammy. "Get it out of your system."

"Your words, Tammy," says Mum reasonably. "I believe that was one of your parting shots as you left home for university almost a year ago."

"Yes, well, I've had almost a year of eating wholemeal pasta with ketchup to think about it," says Tammy.

"And?" says Mum teasingly.

29

"You don't mean…"

"Yes," says Tammy. "I don't say this very often, but I may have been *wrong*."

"I think that might be the first time I've ever heard you say that," says Dad.

Mum folds her arms and looks at Tammy. "So," she says, "you're interested in bourgeois, tasty cooking?"

"No," says Tammy firmly. "I'm interested in how to be economical. That's a genuine skill, Mum. Especially in these hard times."

Weirdest. Dinner. *Ever*. Tammy makes herself a Marmite sandwich (because she's still vegetarian) and joins us at the table. Then her and Mum just keep chatting about how to make shepherd's pie from scratch, while Tammy makes notes on our telephone pad.

Mum and Tammy rarely communicate this positively. Mum actually seems a bit torn. I think part of her is flattered, but it's also putting her slightly on edge.

It's putting me on edge, too. I feel way more secure when everyone is shouting at each other. You know where you are with people then.

"Lamb is a delicious meat," Mum is saying.

"Well, I'll have to use Quorn or soya," replies Tammy, scribbling away.

"That definitely won't taste as nice," I comment.

"*Shhh*," Tammy hisses at me. "Stop interrupting."

"There's ways to get extra flavour in," says Mum. "The secret ingredient is curry powder."

"You put curry powder in shepherd's pie?" I blurt out, surprised.

"Just a tiny bit, not too much," Mum replies.

"I said, stop interrupting!" Tammy snaps at me.

You *know* the world has gone mad when Tammy is snapping at me and listening to Mum. I mean, what next? A green sky and blue grass?

"How are you coming along with my cartoon, big mouth?" Tammy asks me then.

"*Big mouth?*" I'm offended. "I have every right to express surprise at the unexpected presence of curry powder in my tea," I say huffily.

"Have you finished it yet?" says Tammy.

"Nearly," I lie. "I've got a bit more to do after dinner."

"Great." Then she goes back to quizzing Mum.

"Why is Tammy suddenly so into cooking?" I ask my dad later as he washes up, while the rest of the family sit in the living room drinking tea.

"Oh, you know," says Dad evasively. "Sometimes, when you're that blinkered, you find the obvious amazing."

"Daddddddeeeee!" Ryan runs in and grabs Dad's legs, giggling. "*Don't* tickle me!"

"Everyone out." Mum and Tammy enter the kitchen, looking purposeful. "I'm going to *show* Tammy how to make a shepherd's pie."

Why did I say I'd nearly finished? I berate myself as I sit at my desk later, still feeling clueless about what to draw. And why is *everyone* else so down on cartoons?

I can't *believe* Natalie and Amelia's attitude in McDonald's earlier. Or Mum and Dad's yesterday. I mean, I expect that kind of thing from my mum, *sure*. But it seems very hypocritical of my *dad* to join in.

Especially since he was, until recently, living up a *tree*, like some kind of irresponsible lunatic. (He had a sort of mini midlife crisis and joined Tammy on a protest to save the forest.)

Incidentally, while he was "dealing with some issues" (as Mum put it) he was actually very positive about me following my dream of becoming an artist. He kept saying life was too short not to. Now he's got back into being all sensible and into keeping the lawn neat instead.

Which is pretty rich of him, because (a) our lawn is still covered in daisies and dandelions, and (b) while up the tree, he met like-minded people, one of whom offered him a job. And now he has practically his dream position working for the charity Green Fortis.

He's much happier than he was at his old job. And there are some really great perks – free fair trade chocolate for one. The car is a downside, obviously, but you can't have everything.

The car is a bright, luminous shade of lime green, and it has a slogan on the side in big yellow writing, saying "Living the electric dream!" I'm sure it's green to represent the environment, but the choice of colouring does make it feel more like an advert for a fizzy lemon and lime drink.

Dad's transition was kind of like a lesson in not caring about materialistic things, and then being rewarded. So it seems hypocritical to encourage me to get a "good" job that will most likely make me as miserable as he used to be. Though to be fair, he is still more enthusiastic about creativity than Mum.

Eugh. Anyway. *What can I draw that's funny for a political campaign…?* It's got to make people think about global warming and climate change in a whole new way. Oh God, this is hopeless. I lean my head on my desk and moan quietly. *No.* Come on, you *can do this*.

I sit up straight again. OK. OK, so, how do people think about climate change now? Well, according to Tammy, they "can't be bothered to engage with it". So I guess it doesn't seem real to them.

But it won't become *real* until it's the future, and you can't draw the *definite* future, you can only guess at it. (Like how I guessed that aliens will run our school in the future – it *could* happen.) So I could draw the future, where everything will be mostly under water. And that isn't *funny*, it's sad. Unless you're a fish. *Hey*... Unless you're any animal that can swim. Then, not only is it *fine* for you, but there are fewer humans actually trying to *eat* you. *Hmmmm.*

I sit and think a bit more, and let pictures of all kinds of marine life fill my mind. Are they happy? Are they wistful? Do they miss the humans? Is the

sea too crowded if no one goes hunting and fishing?
Surely it would be a paradise for them?

Maybe there'd be a new idiot
animal that's replaced the
humans? Maybe jellyfish
would be the next most
annoying creature, and
everyone would bully
them. Suddenly I'm full of
ideas. But I can't use them all, and
they're not quite right yet. I *love* brainstorming.

As I let my mind free-fall, I realise I had been
coming at the cartoon from the wrong angle. It's not
what's funny about flooding, it's kind of the opposite.
Comedy is tragedy plus time. Or something.

Finally I settle on an idea I like. Two dolphins are
in the sea, talking to each other. One of them says to
the other one, "I remember when all this was fields."

I think, hopefully, it strikes the right note. It's a
twist on that annoying phrase adults say when they're
a) pointing out how old they are, and b) complaining
at the changes modern life has made to where they
live. (My dad says it whenever we drive past the
new housing estate that was built recently over the

countryside at the edge of town.)

The twist is that it's not houses that are covering the fields, but water, because humans didn't look after the environment properly. Hopefully it's funny without being too dark, and the surprise of the juxtaposition will make people think about climate change in a new light.

Phew.

CHAPTER 5

Tammy *loved* the cartoon! God, I feel so much better as I ride the bus to school the next day. I can't believe I let everyone bring me down with their negative attitudes.

Sure, cartoons aren't for *everyone*. But let the people that like them get on with their lives. *Honestly*. All this legacy nonsense. Who cares about leaving a legacy? I'm doing this for *me* and because it's *fun*. I don't need outside validation. (Except from Tammy, it seems.)

Anyway, I really don't care if they all argue with me again. I'm making cartoons my legacy, or I'm not having a legacy, and that's fine with me. *Idiots*. Haha.

I arrive in my form room to find Harriet VanDerk arguing with Amelia and Natalie.

"I really must insist I be allowed to have a *list* of things as my legacy," says Harriet.

"No deal," says Nat. "You have to pick just one."

"But I'm so good at *so many* things, that's impossible!" cries Harriet.

Harriet's sense of her own greatness really winds people up. Including me, even though I try not to let it.

"Well," replies Amelia through gritted teeth, "pick the one you think you're the *best* at."

"You're not listening to me. I'm equally good at *everything* I do!" Harriet is incensed.

"Well, we've explained the situation," says Nat flatly.

"Why don't you make your legacy 'best at everything'?" I joke, dropping my bag on my desk.

"I know you're laughing at me, Jessica." Harriet eyes me critically. "But that's actually not a bad

BEST AT EVERYTHING

idea. How else can I encapsulate my Further Maths, Mandarin, grade 6 piano and excellent exam results?"

Amelia cracks and lapses into sarcasm. "It's hard, isn't it?" she simpers. "You have such a *plethora* of strings to your bow. Maybe you could make your legacy 'overachieving at everything except *art*'?"

Oooh, *burn*! This is a sore spot for Harriet. She's *very* competitive. Not **BURN!** satisfied with being the best at practically everything, she got very annoyed when Mrs Cooper preferred my set designs to hers, and so kept trying to boss me about (even though she had no authority to do so).

"I know what you're trying to do," says Harriet. "But I'm totally over Mrs Cooper's ludicrous choices. There's no accounting for taste. And I totally put it behind me at the time. And I was very supportive of the bad artistic direction the production went in. I should actually add team building and professionalism to my legacy list."

Amelia and I stare open-mouthed at her. I know the VanDerks have a habit of rewriting their own history, but that still really took the biscuit. I mean, it could not have been more *opposite* of what happened.

"That's *funny*." Amelia recovers first. "Because

I remember it as you getting into trouble for constantly sabotaging us, and then being forced to back down."

"Potato potarto," I quip. "Let's not split hairs, Amelia. Sabotaging people is *practically* the same as professionalism."

Natalie and Amelia laugh, which I'm glad about, because Harriet is being very insulting to me. *Again*. Though I do sometimes feel a bit bad when I crack a joke that makes everyone laugh at one person. Even if that one person is mean and deserves it.

"Yeah, laugh it up." Harriet turns on me. "Is that *your* legacy, Jessica? Class clown? The fool, the funny *idiot*? Enjoy it while it lasts, because I'm sure the only reason Mrs Cooper wanted to use your designs in the first place was to make you feel better for being so *rubbish* at everything else!"

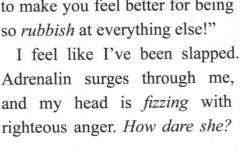

I feel like I've been slapped. Adrenalin surges through me, and my head is *fizzing* with righteous anger. *How dare she?*

But I remain outwardly calm and say, "It's great you really are so over it," making Natalie and Amelia laugh again.

"Yeah? Well, at least I'm not a charity case!" Harriet shoots back.

"Oh, just go away!" Nat shouts at Harriet. "Stop being horrible to Jess."

"Fine, I'm leaving," says Harriet. "I can't believe you two are in charge of the yearbook. It should have been me. I'd be *way* better at it."

"Hey, don't listen to Harriet," says Nat, putting her arm around me. "You're not the class idiot."

"I know," I say, feeling weirdly defensive all of a sudden. Why did she feel the need to point that out?

I don't really think Mrs Cooper chose my designs out of pity. I'm not even *that* rubbish at other subjects. And why would a teacher do that? It seems very unlikely. Mrs Cooper didn't choose my designs for the wrong reasons. Definitely. *Did she?*

God, you'd think everything would get *easier* now that school is winding down, but my life is like a roller coaster at the moment. One minute I'm up and excited because I drew a great dolphin cartoon that

Tammy loved, the next I'm down in the dumps and paranoid I'm a rubbish charity case, thanks to Harriet VanDerk.

I wish I could magic it back to this morning again, when I was elated, before I spoke to Harriet. I wish I could un-hear what she said about Mrs Cooper. But I can't un-hear it, and I can't shake off the feeling that it *could* be true.

I mean, sometimes adults *do* try and spare your feelings a bit. Like, once my mum put a picture Ryan drew of a rocket on the fridge, and you couldn't even tell it was a rocket. It was just sort of some red and yellow squiggles.

Then he spent the rest of that day lording it over me, saying I wasn't the only artist in the family. When I complained Mum just told me, "Oh, let him have his moment, he's younger than you." So adults *do* sometimes pretend they're more impressed with kids than they really are, to help their self-esteem. Is *that* what this was? Was my set design actually *my fridge rocket*?

No. It can't be. But... *No*, it can't be. But... Aaaarrgghh. I *hate* Harriet VanDerk.

Afternoon lessons on Thursdays are "free time" so people can finish off other projects they're doing or play about with the graphics packages on the computers. I sit with Natalie and Amelia and help them with the yearbook.

"Most likely to become a pop star?" suggests Natalie.

"Yep, good one." Amelia nods approval and writes it down.

"Most likely to steal the Crown Jewels?" I say. Nat chuckles; Amelia writes it down. "Most likely to be abducted by aliens?" I offer.

44

"You're obsessed with aliens," comments Amelia.

"It's funny, though," says Nat. Amelia writes it down.

"Ooh, put most likely to win an Oscar," says Nat. "That's me, I'm most likely to win an Oscar."

"Can you decide that?" I ask.

"Of course, I'm on the committee," replies Nat.

"The committee of you two?" I query.

"Yes. But I *was* just the *lead* in the school musical, Jess."

"Oh, *were* you? I'd completely forgotten; it was so uneventful and you never talk about it."

Nat laughs and hits my arm affectionately. "Oi."

"Hi, guys," says Cherry, coming over with Shantair. They're my friends from the chess club. They're shy and clever, and get annoyed when I try to talk to them during lessons.

"We've just printed out our yearbook pictures on the computers for you." Shantair hands them over.

"Wow, cool picture of you as the Cowardly Lion!" I say to her. "You look great."

"Thanks!" Shantair beams shyly. I was concerned

she was typecast as the Cowardly Lion, but she really was very good. She does drama outside school.

Cherry's picture is of her winning the chess championship cup last week. "You might as well make that my legacy thing too, I guess," she says.

"Sure thing," says Nat, as Amelia takes the photos carefully.

"Nice one!" I enthuse supportively, while my stomach lurches. I still don't have a committee-approved legacy. I'm pretty good at chess but I'm still not good enough at it that it's my *thing*.

They head back over to their computer and we go back to trying to come up with more *most-likely-to*'s. We think we should give everyone a "nice" (boring, normal) one, and a funny one, so that no one can get offended. I rattle off whatever comes into my head (there's no judgment in blue sky) and soon we have an impressive list:

Most likely to fall down a manhole
Most likely to win a hot-dog-eating competition
Most likely to fall asleep on the bus
Most likely to sing in the shower
Most likely to win a Nobel Prize
Most likely to win *X Factor*

Most likely to become a teacher

Most likely to get caught eating sweets in a lesson

Most likely to break a world record (for farting)

Most likely to become a comedian

Most likely to win the lottery but lose the ticket

Most likely to have a town named after them

Most likcly to discover they have a secret twin

We're giggling at "most likely to get accidentally locked in a toilet" (which Nat thinks might be too mean to include) when my friends Emily, Megan and Fatimah come over with their pictures. They're my friends that love messing about in lessons, and love it when I start talking to them when we're meant to be learning.

All their photos are really good, too. Fatimah's picture is of her holding a really cute kitten, which makes Natalie squeal with delight. Emily is sitting on a high wall with a lovely blue sky behind her, and Megan's picture is of her at Harry Potter World, grinning and sticking her thumbs up.

"Brilliant, thanks. Do you have your legacies

worked out?" asks Amelia.

"Oh, uh, yeah, all right then," says Emily. "How about this?" And with that, she sticks her whole fist in her mouth.

Amelia gapes at her. Natalie says, really slowly, "Wow!"

I'd forgotten Emily could do this, and I can't help but chuckle at Amelia's reaction. I know this is not the kind of thing Amelia finds impressive, as she's still a little snooty, and I'm sure that she's finding it somewhat uncouth.

"You want ... *that* to be your legacy?" Amelia queries.

"Yeah. Is that not the kind of thing you mean?" asks Emily. "I bet no one else can do it."

"That's true," says Megan. She and Fatimah immediately start trying to fit their fists in their mouths, and I join in for good measure.

"Itsssff fthrilly harrrd," I garble, removing my fist again.

"OK, if you're sure," Amelia says politely, and makes a note. "What about you two?"

"I've got the neatest handwriting," says Fatimah.

"And I won the hundred metres on sports day," beams Megan. "I even beat the boys. My legacy is *speed*."

"Those are all such good legacies," I say with awe.

"What's yours?" Emily asks. "Inventing the *would you rather* game?"

"Ha, I *wish*," I say. "I didn't invent it; I played it somewhere else and then brought it to our school."

"You could have *popularising* the *would you rather* game?" Amelia looks up from making notes.

"OK, everyone!" says Mrs Cole. "If I could have your attention, please. Start finishing off what you're doing and logging off your computers."

"Ooh, gotta go." Emily, Megan and Fatimah swiftly head back to their work terminal to log out.

"Are you seriously *still* not letting me have cartoons?" I ask Amelia and Natalie. "Emily's legacy is fitting her fist in her mouth."

"Well, as she said, she *is* the only one that can do it," points out Nat. "Lots of other people can draw cartoons."

Un-be-*lievable*.

49

CHAPTER 6

I think I might have sighed so much on my way home that I sprained my oesophagus.

SIGH And I sigh again as I open the front SIGH door, and then feel slightly cheered up by Lady, who lies at my feet, blocking my way, trying to convince me to tickle her tummy. So I do.

I *really* don't see why Natalie and Amelia can't just let me have cartoons as my legacy. I know I haven't won a *prize* for them, and I can't be *empirically* proved the best or whatever (like Cherry with her chess championship cup) but I'm the one that likes cartoons the most. Surely that should count for something?

I think they're just being pig-headed and don't

want to back down now. The pig-headed … *pigs*. (Yeah, I went there.)

"You did *what*?" I hear my mum shout from the kitchen.

"Calm down." This time it's Tammy doing the placating, not my dad. Where's my dad? He's going to need to make my mum an all-calming cup of tea *immediately. Stat.*

"Cup of tea?" I hear his voice. *Phew*.

Well, the ceasefire didn't last long. I wonder if I dare to enter the kitchen and find out what happened. But it turns out I don't need to.

"You had *no business* putting the recipes I gave you on a public blog for all the world to see!" Mum exclaims.

"But it's to help people!" Tammy seems incredulous. "You're an expert at feeding a family healthy food on a shoestring budget. Loads of people would love to know how to do that. Don't you want to share your experience with the needy?"

"Why didn't you ask me first?"

"I didn't think you'd object!"

"I don't want a bunch of weirdos on the Internet knowing my business; it's not safe!"

"Tea's on its way!" Dad interjects, trying to sound cheerful, but actually sounding a bit strained.

"Yeah, it's *so unsafe*," shouts Tammy sarcastically. "Especially since I put your name, address and bank details up there as well."

"What?!"

"Obviously I'm joking." Tammy quickly backs down on that one. Even she can see there's no point pushing Mum over the edge.

"Tea!" My dad's triumphant yell finally drowns them both out. "Why don't we have a nice sit-down and talk about this *sensibly*."

I hear the kitchen chairs being scraped across the floor and decide it's safe to go in.

Lady follows me, then sits down and yawns loudly. My mum, dad and Tammy are now sitting at the table in front of the laptop.

"Why don't you have a look at the blog

before you dismiss it out of hand?" Tammy is saying.

I hear my mum mutter something that sounds like "living end", but she sips tea and looks thoughtful.

"Oh, there she is!" Tammy says excitedly, spotting me. "The woman of the hour!"

"What have *I* done?" I ask suspiciously, not sure I want to look so much like Tammy's ally when Mum is still annoyed with her.

"Your cartoon has gone viral, you little beauty!" Tammy sounds absolutely delighted, all righteous anger forgotten. "I *knew* you could do it."

"What do you mean it's 'gone viral'?" I ask.

"It's the number-one thing on Newsworth."

"What on earth's Newsworth?" asks Mum, getting ready to be concerned about my online safety.

Tammy rolls her eyes. "Must I always be the one dragging this family kicking and screaming into the twenty-first century? It's a user-generated website for entertainment and news links. Votes promote stories to the front page. So only the most popular stories and links get the attention. Over a million people a month use it. Jessica has just made *thousands* of people more aware of climate change!"

"I… I have?" I think I need to sit down. I mean, *what*?

"You're famous!" Tammy beams. "On the Internet."

"No, no, no," says Mum, shaking her head. "Jessica is far too young to be famous on the Internet."

"Don't worry, you'll be famous too, once I get this blog running properly," says Tammy, missing the point.

"You know that isn't what I mean," says Mum tersely, as she sips more tea.

I sit down. My head is spinning. My cartoon has been *shared on the Internet*? Loads of people have seen it? They've seen my work? That's incredible. I thought it might end up on a few flyers or something, but … the Internet!

"Yeah, good, sit down. I'll show you in a sec," says Tammy. "I'll just show Mum this first. Right, so this is the page."

"Oh, *really*?" Mum sounds more pleased than angry now. "That's quite pretty. I like the colour scheme."

"Good." Tammy smiles. "I've called it *Budget Family Food Made Simple*," she continues.

"I like how you've done the letters a bit swirly," says Mum.

Budget Family Food made Simple.

"Great." Tammy tries not to look too pleased with herself, like a parent that has just tricked an infant into eating their greens. "There's three recipes up there now."

Tammy goes through everything with Mum, who is actively delighted with most of it. But she's a bit embarrassed that Tammy has revealed her "top tip for budget buying", which is knowing exactly what time the food gets reduced at the supermarket and waiting till then to buy it.

"But that's genius," insists Tammy. "It's maybe sad that it's *necessary* in today's climate," she adds, "but you shouldn't be embarrassed. It's the fat cats who've caused the crisis who should be."

"Always with the fat cats," comments Dad.

Tammy ignores him. "Right, wanna see what your superstar eleven-year-old has done?" she asks.

I step round the table so I can see what she's clicking on. It's my cartoon! Online! With some information about the climate-change campaign it's supporting and the fact that it was drawn by an eleven-year-old from our town.

There are a couple of comments underneath, and

LoL!

they say things like, "LOL! So true," and "I can't believe this was drawn by an eleven-year-old!" I can't see any others. I've heard bad things about "the bottom half of the Internet" but this all seems very positive so far.

Oh my God, I'm *online*. I'm making people LOL! People outside my classroom. This is *amazing*. This is everything I ever dreamed of. I have achieved my life's goal at the age of eleven. I can retire now. I don't want to sound big-headed or anything, but bloody hell, *I'm amazing*! **amazING!**

Everyone is speechless for a moment as we look at the screen. Then my dad says, "I'm very proud of you, Jessica." It makes me feel strangely emotional. So I figure it's not the time to make a cheap shot about how they told me to stop drawing,

56

and how wrong they were.

"We're *all* very proud of you," agrees Mum. She's a lot more relaxed now that Tammy has explained that she hasn't put my name anywhere and no one can get in touch with me.

"So proud!" beams Tammy. "It's funny *and* it's helped raise awareness of the issues. Result!"

CHAPTER 7

This is so weird. My family's never been *proud* of me before. Weary, *yes*. Uncomfortable, *sure*. Apologetic, *of course*. But *proud* is a whole new thing.

I mean, they've *said* they were proud in the past. But then they *had* to say that, didn't they? It would be *mean* to tell your nine-year-old that the choice of green icing made their fairy cakes look like lumps of slime, and that's why they sold badly at the cake sale for the old people's home. 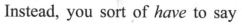 Instead, you sort of *have* to say that they were "so perfect" no one wanted to "spoil them by eating them", and that you're *very proud*

58

of said nine-year-old. (I am the nine-year-old in this scenario.)

I've come a long way since my green-cake fiasco. This time it's like they really mean it. And even if they didn't mean it, a whole bunch of strangers do. I am an Internet-endorsed *satirist*!

"Oh, hi, guys!" I address Natalie and Amelia casually in class the next morning.

"You sound happy," observes Nat.

"*Meee?*" I'm very bad at hiding my glee, to be fair.

"Yes, you." Nat raises an inquisitive eyebrow at me.

"Well, it's like you said the other day in McDonald's," I say. "The sky is blue and we've got our whole lives ahead of us."

"And?" prompts Amelia. "So?"

"Oh, I don't know," I say evasively, running my finger around my desk. "Just a little thing I like to call *massive, unbelievable success in my chosen career!*" I drop the blasé act and almost end up garbling that last bit as I'm so excited.

"What? What's happened?" Nat looks pleased but confused.

I quickly pull out a printed screenshot of my cartoon on the home page of Newsworth. I thought it would be easier to bring that in rather than try and load the page on my phone. And it would be embarrassing if I'd already been replaced by a dog dressed as a spider or a sneezing panda or something.

"What's all this then?" asks Amelia.

I explain, in quite a lot of detail, about how my satirical cartoon has become an Internet sensation. I'm looking forward to pointing out that perhaps drawing cartoons *can* be a worthy legacy after all, while not actually rubbing their faces in it or anything. I can be very gracious like that.

"That's *really cool*, Jess!" cries Nat.

"I know!" I squeal. "Isn't it? I'm so excited. I still can't believe it."

"I thought you'd got a scholarship somewhere, or something," says Amelia.

"What?" I say surprised.

"I mean, when you said something about a *career*—" She clocks my face and quickly says, "No but this is good too! That's great you drew a thing and posted it to a website."

"I didn't just … that's not what—"

"You are *so good* at drawing dolphins!" interrupts Nat, as if to appease me.

"It's not just the dolphins, it's the whole *thing*," I say. Haven't they been *listening*? Don't they get that it's *satire*? "And *I* didn't upload it, my sister did. It's part of a campaign. Other people – strangers – voted it the number-one thing on that website. *Thousands* of people like it!"

"All right, all right, we'll let you put drawing cartoons as your legacy," says Amelia, chuckling and shaking her head. As if that's what this *whole thing* has been about. When really that's at least only *half* of what it's been about.

"Look, I didn't do this for my stupid legacy!" I say crossly.

"All right, don't have drawing cartoons then," says Amelia.

"No, look." (How has this gone so badly?) "I'll take cartoons as my legacy." (If you don't mind, thank you very much.) "But I didn't make *thousands* of people like my cartoon just to impress you. It just happened and I think that's cool."

"We do too, Jess," says Nat, smiling.

"Yes, it's cool," says Amelia. Unconvincingly.

Honestly. What's *wrong* with these people? I mean, to be fair, Natalie seems suitably impressed. But Amelia is a bit of a killjoy. I suppose she's never really seen the point of drawing cartoons, though.

At least Joshua and Tanya will be pleased for me. *They'll* understand the significance. They'll appreciate that I am a genius of gigantic proportions who is setting the Internet ON FIRE.

"Oh my God! That's *amazing*!" exclaims Joshua.

See?

"*Brilliant!*" agrees Tanya. "That's epic, Toons!"

I *knew* it. Proper reactions.

"High five!" says Joshua. He high-fives me.

"Thanks," I reply, unable to stop grinning.

"Blimey," says Lewis more sedately, but I think that means he's impressed, too. He very rarely compliments me.

"I always said you was talented, right from day one," states Tanya.

"So cool!" Joshua grins.

"I *know*!" I just about manage not to squeal again. I'm so happy. I love it when everyone thinks I'm brilliant, because I've done something brilliant. It's probably one of my favourite things.

"It's bizarre, though," says Lewis. "Who would have thought some random dolphins would be so popular?"

Random dolphins? God, don't be *too* happy for me, Lewis, I think sarcastically. "Well, I guess people like dolphins," I say modestly. Not to mention my *biting wit*, I add secretly. It's really great how self-effacing and grounded I still am.

"I would have thought robots or something would be more popular," Lewis continues to muse. Lewis draws quite a lot of robots, now I think about it. Maybe he's *jealous*.

I REMEMBER WHEN ALL THIS WAS FIELDS!

"Don't worry, Lewis, your time will come," I say sweetly. Lewis scowls at me before he manages to control his face.

"The whole thing might be a bit *odd*," he says, looking right at me. "But I think it'll be great for the comic."

"The comic?" I query.

"Oh *yeah*!" cries Tanya. "Not just a hat rack, eh, Lewis? Good thinking. This *could* be really great publicity for the comic!"

"Yeah, it could really help us," nods Joshua. "Well done, Lewis."

Whoa, whoa, whoa. Really great **HELLo?** publicity for *them*? Well done, *Lewis*? Who is the genius here? I mean, *hello*? This is *my* moment.

I let them have *their* moment when they were acting in *The Wizard*. I said things like, "Well done, Joshua, you were really funny as the Scarecrow," and "That was amazing, Tanya, you're hilarious!"

What I *didn't* do was immediately follow that up with, "Hey, maybe you could plug issue six in the middle of your monologue? Eyes on the prize, guys."

Why do they have to make this *all about them*?

Why can't they just tell me I'm brilliant for five minutes? (Although, to be fair, they have said that.) But why can't they say it *a bit more* before they start asking for favours?

"It's a really great cartoon," says Lewis.

"Thank you," I reply graciously. That's more like it. Maybe I have been a bit quick to judge.

"How did you load it up there?" he asks.

"I don't know. My sister posted it on the site."

"Find out how she did it," says Lewis bossily.

"Good thinking," says Tanya. "Gather the info, Toons."

"Uh-huh," I say as politely as I can. "Why, exactly?"

Joshua carries on as if I haven't spoken. "Guys, we should think very carefully about how we launch ourselves online. I'm not sure we're completely ready yet."

"I say we strike while the iron is hot," says Tanya. "It's good PR and that. We can say 'From the girl who brought you the dolphin cartoon comes a brand-new online comic' or something. You know."

"Yeah, actually, that's good," says Joshua.

So that's what my cartoon is, is it? *A marketing tool?* I can't help but feel slightly sidelined.

"Oh, well done, Toons!" Tanya claps me hard on the back, making me cough. "You never cease to amaze me! You're always on. You're a maverick, you are. Always full of surprises. I love it."

And that does make me feel better. Maybe I'm overreacting. Maybe it's fair enough that a successful cartoon by one of us should help plug all of us. Maybe I'd expect it too if it was the other way round.

And they couldn't really plug the comic in the middle of the school musical, could they? So that *is* different. I might really be able to make a difference to the comic's fortunes. And that's quite cool. And also, it kind of gives me power. Not that I care about that kind of thing.

"It's lucky your dolphin cartoon suits our brand," says Lewis then.

What? Why can't he just stop talking?

My dolphin cartoon – if it is anyone's brand – is *my* brand. And, some might say (and they might be right) that the *comic* is *my brand* because it was my funny cartoons that set the tone of the whole thing. Not the other way round. I mean, Tanya kind of guided me a *bit*, but *still*.

And then I hear myself say that out loud. "Actually, Lewis, I don't think it's 'our brand'. I think it's my *unique* brand that *luckily for you* I bring to the comic as well."

Everyone pauses for a microsecond. I guess that did sound kind of arrogant. Slightly.

"Right. Yeah," says Tanya, narrowing her eyes at me before deciding to let it go. "It's all brilliant branding. OK, Toons, so you should plug us every chance you get. Interviews, what have you. Plug our comic. We can start the whisper campaign, get people interested."

"Interviews?" I query.

"Whatever comes up," nods Tanya.

"OK," I promise dutifully. Ha, as if I'll be giving *interviews*. I love Tanya's optimism, though.

"This is gonna be great, Toons!" Tanya beams.

"Yeah!" I agree. It is. I'm *great*. That's the main take-home message here.

And I'm more than happy to plug the comic if any opportunities present themselves. After all, I love the comic. I'm a big, successful person now. I have a responsibility to help the little guy. I'm definitely going to be one of those nice famous people you sometimes hear about, the ones who don't forget where they started. It's all about roots.

CHAPTER 8

"Monster attack!" Ryan rolls over on the living-room floor and grabs my feet.

"Attack, Lady, attack! Eat the feet!" he commands the dog, who rolls over as well and starts sniffing my feet.

"*Ryan*," I say tiredly, removing my legs from the theatre of conflict and tucking them under me on the sofa. "I'm *trying* to watch TV."

"She's getting away! After her!" Ryan jumps up next to me and encourages Lady to do the same by patting the sofa. Lady jumps up and sits on my other side.

"Ryan, Mum doesn't let Lady on the sofa, remember?"

Lady promptly gets herself comfy and lies down with her head in my lap, looking wistful. It's really cute, and obviously I'm in no mood to move her now.

"Lady, you're a rubbish monster," sighs Ryan. At least he's stopped putting the space helmet on her. Though to be fair, she didn't seem to mind.

I stroke Lady's head. "She's my monster now," I tell him.

"Never!" cries my little brother. "I'll get you, and you should know that the only thing that can stop me is being tickled, so whatever you do, don't tickle me."

Oh great, not *this* again. "OK," I say.

"I mean it," insists Ryan. "Don't tickle me, Jessica."

"I won't."

"*Ever*," he adds. "No tickling."

"Fine," I say. Then, "What, you mean like this?" and I start tickling him with my free hand.

He squeals with delight and rolls out of the way where I can't reach him. Then we hear my mother calling from the kitchen. *Uh-oh, what now?*

"Dinner's nearly ready, kids, so why don't you do something useful like lay the table? I just need to finish something on the computer."

Hey. What's *Mum* doing on the computer? I clamber off the sofa and head into the kitchen, where Ryan has made a start on chucking cutlery on to the table.

I look at the computer curiously, and see it's open on the food blog that Tammy set up. Mum is looking at her *own* Web page. *Hmmm.*

"Going well, is it?" I ask, nodding at the computer.

"What do you mean?" Mum looks confused for a second. "Oh, this? Yes, *actually*." She beams proudly. "It's had *rather a lot* of hits, if you must know. And some lovely comments. I'm quite the chef about town, it seems."

"That's great, Mum," I say. "So what's for dinner?"

"Hmm? Oh, tuna pie. It's off the website."

71

I've seen Mum make this. It's literally tinned tuna, tinned soup and crisps all mixed together. Sometimes she adds sweetcorn if she's feeling flashy, and then it all goes into the  oven. It's definitely one of the more budget dishes from her budget range.

"Has it gone down well?" I enquire.

"Very," says Mum.

I suppose if the aim is to spend as little as possible, the tuna pie *is* going to be impressive. It's not about Michelin stars, it's about maximising profit per square nutrient. Or something.

And to be fair, I actually really like Mum's tuna pie. I just don't want her to get too big-headed. She already has quite an inflated sense of her own importance. You'd never catch me doing that.

The phone rings and Mum goes to answer it, muttering darkly about people who move the telephone pad being the living end. . .

"Yes, hello? Yes. Really? *Really?* Well… I'm not sure. I'll have to ask her. And discuss it. Yes, do give me your number." Then she mouths to us, "Get me a pad *now*!" Ryan hands Mum a water bill. "OK, yes. I've got it, thanks. Bye."

"What was all that about?" I ask, finishing putting out the plates.

"That was the local paper," says Mum, looking a bit shell-shocked. "They've heard about your cartoon. They want to run a little feature on you."

Oh my God, *oh my God*. The local paper wants to run a feature on *me*! I'm staying totally cool about this and not letting it go to my head at all.

OK, so I *have* been picturing how Nat, Amelia, Harriet VanDerk, my comic friends and basically everyone at school will look when they find out that I am a superstar, but apart from that, I'm staying totally cool about it.

What's nice as well is that my family are being uncharacteristically cool about it. They're really impressed and proud of me! It's such a weird feeling. Dinner has become a discussion all about me.

I mean, Mum does seem to be a bit preoccupied with the idea that I'm too young to have my picture in the paper, but I'm sure the publicity agent I'm clearly going to need to hire soon can talk her round. Haha, joking. Mainly joking anyway. I might need a publicity agent soon. You never know.

"Mum, I've already been in the paper once when Dad went up that tree, remember?"

"That was different, that was all of us together," says Mum. "I'm just worried you might be a

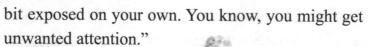

bit exposed on your own. You know, you might get unwanted attention."

"I like the attention," I say. "I like it when people like my cartoons."

"That isn't quite what I—"

"I think it should be Jessica's decision," interrupts Dad. "It's only the local paper; it'll be tomorrow's fish and chips wrappers anyway."

I'm going to assume Dad is saying that for Mum's benefit and not to belittle my glorious achievement.

"Actually, things stay online forever now," replies Mum.

Honestly, one food blog and she thinks she's an expert on the Internet. Two days ago she didn't even know what a meme was.

"Can I have fish and chips?" says Ryan.

"Ryan, you're already eating fish," I point out.

"And what about Ryan?" Mum leaps on this. "We don't want him to feel left out, do we?"

"*Mum*," I say tiredly, trying not to sound too annoyed. "You can't make me share *everything* with Ryan for the rest of my *life*. What if I become Prime Minister, would you try to make me job-share with Ryan?"

"You'll have to start working *much* harder at school if you want to become Prime Minister," scoffs Mum, never off duty from getting in a dig about my school report.

"Let's not get too far off the subject," says Dad. "I think this is a wonderful thing that has happened to our talented daughter, and a cause for celebration."

That's more like it.

"I know it is," agrees Mum. "I think that too, of course. I'm just a bit worried about, you know... There's a downside to fame. And Jessica is still so young."

"*Muuuuum*," I implore.

"Well," says Mum. "I'm going to call Joan and see what *she* thinks."

CHAPTER 9

Of course Auntie Joan thinks I should do it! Has Mum even *met* her own sister? Once upon a time Joan would have immediately taken the opposite view to my dad, but Auntie Joan loves Dad since he lived up a tree.

Joan is very much from the "showing spirit = being brilliant" school of thought. I think her scorn for authority has definitely influenced Tammy. Anyway, I don't mind because Auntie Joan is loads of fun. And she's also the reason that my mum says yes, I can do the newspaper interview! **YES !!**

Joan even wants to come and help "prepare" me. She does publicity and admin for a national orchestra and so she knows all about how these things are meant to go down. I think Mum felt reassured that Joan would be in charge. And I told you I'd need to hire a publicist!

Mum's only other complaint was that it might be "too much" for me to do a newspaper interview in the same week we get to go and visit our new school. But as I pointed out, she had no trouble making us walk for six miles when we got lost once in Cornwall, and that was much harder, if you think about it.

Anyway. Totes normal as I ride the bus to school the next day. Definitely going to play it cool with everyone, as if I get asked to be in the local paper because of my awesome cartooning every day.

"Oh my God, you won't believe what's happening!" I all but yell as I enter my form room and startle Natalie and Amelia out of yet another yearbook discussion. Well, I *almost* played it cool. Slightly stumbled at the very last *playing it cool* hurdle there.

"Jeez, Jess, give us a heart attack, why don't you?" says Nat crossly, as I bound over to them.

I summon all the self-control I can muster, and exclaim as unsqueakily as I can, "I'm going to be interviewed in the local paper about that dolphin cartoon I did! Can you believe it?"

"*Really?*" says Amelia, slightly incredulously, I have to say.

"Yep!" I reply joyfully. "Isn't it amazing!"

"It certainly is," she says.

"That's great, Jess, very exciting!" says Nat.

I beam.

"When will it be out?" asks Amelia.

"Next week, I think," I reply. "I expect they want to strike while the iron is hot, you know. I'm very zeitgeisty."

"Indeed," says Amelia, unconvinced. "Well, that's actually really good timing."

"Why?" I ask.

"Well, there's hardly any of school left, so if it's like a bad photo or something you won't get bullied. And then, by the time we start secondary school, no one will remember it anyway."

"God, I'm so nervous about visiting our secondary school!" exclaims Natalie.

"I *know*," says Amelia.

"Why would it be a bad photo?" I stammer.

"It probably won't be," says Amelia. "I'm just saying *if*."

Hmmmm.

"I'm sure they'll take a great photo, Jess," Nat assures me. "You don't have anything to be embarrassed about."

"I'm not embarrassed, I'm excited," I declare, wilting.

"That's the spirit," says Nat.

"I'm not bothered about photos anyway," I assert. "I might pull a funny face, for all I care."

"I wouldn't," says Amelia.

"You so won't," giggles Nat. "When it comes to it you'll totally chicken out."

"I bet you five pounds you won't do it," chips in Amelia.

"You're on," I tell them. "I am a *creative*. I live outside society's rules."

"Your mum will never let you." Nat is really giggling now.

She might have a point there. Also I suppose it *might* be nice to have a nice photo. Especially if I'm holding the cartoon I drew. Maybe that could even be my photo for the yearbook?

I mean, I don't want to cut my nose off to spite my face. Or pull a face so weird it *looks* like someone has cut my nose off and my face is spited. *Hmmm.*

"Well, we'll see," I say. "It might not be up to me. I might have to take artistic direction from the official photographer. Because an official photographer is taking my picture."

I'm not sure but I think I see Amelia roll her eyes. Ha. Jealous.

Natalie and Amelia really do seem quite nervous about the upcoming trip to look around our new school, but I'm genuinely excited. I mean, it is huge and scary and intimidating and all that, but still, *exciting*. Lots of the best things are scary, too.

And they have vending machines. Tammy told me. You can buy cans of Coke there. How amazing is that? To be fair, Tammy doesn't think that's amazing, because she's anti-corporations. But *I* think it means I've arrived.

"No way! That's amazing! I can't believe it," exclaims Joshua as we sit outside the library.

"I can," says Tanya. "I totally predicted this with my business acumen, innit."

"Well done, Jessica," says Lewis politely. Ha. Jealous, too.

It's so fun telling people about my impending local newspaper fame.

"Right then," says Tanya. "We'd better prep you."

"Prep me?"

"Let's go over all the things you need to mention about the comic. You're the public face of our brand now, remember?"

"I am?"

"Course. You said you'd plug us in interviews and that."

"Oh, yes, right, OK." Though to be fair, I didn't think there would *be* any interviews then. It's already snowballed.

"I think you should big up the comedy side of it," advises Joshua. "People love funny things; that will get people interested."

"Yeah," agrees Tanya. "And say that we're entrepreneurs; that makes us sound good too."

"OK," I agree. "Um, what if they don't really want to talk about the comic? I mean, I'll probably have to answer *their* questions, won't I?" (And also talk about *me*.)

"That's why you gotta use your *skilz*, Toons," instructs Tanya. "Make like you're Megan Flyer flogging your new tunes on a chat show."

"Sure, um, I think," I say non-committally.

"Joshua and I will show you," says Tanya. "Joshy-boy, ask us a question."

"Where do you get your crazy ideas from?" asks Joshua.

"Well," answers Tanya, "I work on a comic with three other people and sometimes we all come up with ideas together. Our comic is great. It's launching online soon etc. etc."

"But that *isn't* how I get my crazy ideas," I say.

"Not the point, Toons," replies Tanya. "You gotta stay on-message. Joshua, another one."

"How did you feel when you found out your cartoon had been voted to the top of the website Newsworth?" asks Joshua.

"Really great," answers Tanya. "I was nearly as excited as the day I decided to launch a hilarious

84

online comic with my school friends. Do you get it yet?"

"Yes," I reply. "I think I get the picture. It's, um … not very *subtle*, is it?"

"Not meant to be," reasons Tanya. "That's capitalism for ya."

I have to say, I think these guys are slightly taking the biscuit. But luckily for them, I'm feeling pretty magnanimous about it. I haven't lost touch with my roots; I still remember what it was like before I hit the big time. I'll throw these kids a bone.

CHAPTER 10

"OK, I think that's them! They're here!" calls out Dad excitedly. "Ready?"

"Yes, yes," I say, feeling everyone is making slightly too much fuss about this.

Mum and Auntie Joan talked for literally twenty minutes about what top I should wear. I wanted to wear my favourite one but Mum thinks it's too small. Then Auntie Joan said that was the fashion, and Mum said, "Jessica doesn't care about fashion," which I did sort of have to agree with.

But then it turned into a discussion

about how Mum should buy me more clothes, so I don't have to wear things that are too small. And then Mum got quite annoyed with Auntie Joan, and accused her of having no idea how quickly children grow. Then my dad made everyone a cup of tea.

I hear Dad saying, "Come through, come right this way" in his telephone voice as he ushers the photographer and journalist into the living room, where the rest of us are waiting. Mum did extra hoovering, especially. "Jessica, this is Pamela and this is Greg the photographer, from the paper."

We all shake hands and Dad establishes that everyone wants tea, before disappearing into the kitchen.

"Hello, I'm Ryan." My brother offers his hand to be shaken as well. Pamela and Greg politely oblige, and everyone sits down.

"This is Lady," Ryan continues his introductions. "She's a family dog, but she's more mine really."

"That's nice," says Pamela.

"OK, Ryan." Mum signals for Ryan to go over and sit next to her. He ignores her.

"She likes me the best," he explains. "Lady can shake your hand too if you like?"

"Ryan," repeats Mum.

"Hang on, Mum," says Ryan crossly. "Lady: shake." Lady does nothing. "Sometimes you have to help her." He picks up Lady's paw and places it in the journalist's hand. "There you go. See? She can shake."

"Yeah, really impressive, Ryan," I say. "Next stop, Crufts."

Pamela and Greg smile.

"Well, she can *roll over* on command," continues Ryan. "Mostly."

"Ryan, come and sit here with me, please," says Mum more forcefully. "These nice people haven't come to see you play with Lady, they've come to interview Jessica about her cartoon."

"They probably want to see Lady *a bit* though," reasons Ryan, but he does at least go over to my mum this time. "You haven't asked them what *they* want."

"Lady is a lovely dog," pipes up Pamela, "but your mum's right; we've really come to talk to Jessica."

"OK," says Ryan reasonably. "You can interview me about Lady afterwards if you like."

"We'll see. If there's time," says Pamela kindly.

"I can tell you all about how I trained her," Ryan carries on.

I know I'm supposed to be making a good impression on the journalist and not quarrelling with Ryan or anything, but my head is exploding with what an idiot he's being.

"What *training*, Ryan?" I blurt out. "You've just presented her as the amazing dog that doesn't do *anything* she's told."

"She knows her name," he argues. "Lady!"

Instead of looking round or wagging her tail, Lady makes a noise that sounds like a sigh, and then lies down. "She's just tired," says Ryan apologetically.

"Well, I bet no one can wait to get tickets to the live show," I say sarcastically. "Ryan and the dog who feels tired."

Everyone chuckles. I feel a tiny bit bad and hope I haven't actually upset Ryan. But then he *is* being annoying.

"So, Jessica," says Pamela, turning to me at last. "What is it that inspires you to draw cartoons?" She gets out her pad and presses a button on a tiny tape recorder.

"Well," I reply, "I love comedy. My hero is Matt Groening. I want to be a cartoonist when I grow up. In fact, I already work on a comic with my friends—"

"Oh sorry, I'm not sure this thing is working. Does that light look on to you?" interrupts Pamela.

"Um. Kind of," I say.

"You know what, I'll use my phone. You're happy to be recorded?" She asks this of the room in general. Joan, Mum and I nod. Pamela gets out her phone and fiddles with it. "So you were saying, you like Matt Groening?"

"He's my hero," I say again. "I want to be a funny cartoonist just like him when I grow up. Apart from *The Simpsons* and *Futurama*, he draws comic strips of rabbits that are really funny. In fact, I've actually already set up a comic with some school friends—"

"Tea!" Dad re-enters the room with a tray of tea and biscuits.

"Oh, lovely," says Greg the photographer.

Pamela fiddles with her phone again and Dad starts delightedly serving everyone. We have splashed out on two *different* types of biscuit, after all.

"I tell you what, shall I do the photos while everyone's drinking tea?" asks Greg.

"That's a good idea," says Pamela, biting happily into a chocolate digestive. She has no idea how lucky she is we're over our belt-tightening phase.

Greg takes a few close-up pictures of me holding up a piece of paper with a screen grab of my cartoon at the top of Newsworth, and then Ryan starts acting up again.

"Mummy, I don't think it's fair that *Lady* isn't in the picture," he whines. "I think she feels left out."

Yeah *sure*, I think. *Lady* feels left out. Honestly, Ryan is so transparent.

"Lady's fine, Ryan," says Mum.

"She's *sad*," protests Ryan. "You're making her feel sad."

"I tell you what," says Greg. "It might be nice to get a bit more of a family *action shot*, as it were. Perhaps one of the children and the dog sitting together on the carpet, drawing pictures?"

"That's a lovely idea," says Auntie Joan.

"OK," I say. Ryan is lucky I'm so selfless and happy to share my moment of glory with him. "Do you know where the colouring stuff is, Ryan?" I ask.

"Yes, I'll go and get it." Ryan leaps up and disappears from the room in a flash, forgetting instantly how *sad* Lady is.

Soon Ryan and I are sitting cross-legged on the floor surrounded by paper and pens, with Lady lying next to us. Ryan and I have to "act natural" but pretend I'm teaching him to draw, so I end up showing him how to draw Homer Simpson.

I think Pamela and Greg are quite impressed with my skills. And Ryan behaves perfectly the whole rest of the time.

CHAPTER II

"It comes out tomorrow," I tell Natalie and Amelia as we sit down in the coach that's taking us to our new school for the day. We managed to find seats right at the back, so we can all sit together.

"I'm so nervous," breathes Nat.

"Don't be, I'm sure I'll come out of it looking great," I quip.

"Not your stupid interview – visiting our new school!" replies Nat.

"I know, I'm joking," I say, disappointed to have to explain this. I know that it was a naff joke, but I thought Nat would at least appreciate I'm trying to cheer her up and distract her from her nerves.

We've been allowed to wear home clothes and

everything, which I am very pleased about. I love a mufti day.

"We're all in the same boat," says Amelia.

"Yeah," I agree.

"Well, you say that," says Nat, "but I think, because I'm an *actress*, I'm quite sensitive. So I think I feel things more deeply than you two. It's harder for me."

Amelia and I look at each other and roll our eyes. I fight the urge to giggle. Natalie is really sticking with this whole *actress* thing. I thought she might chill out once the musical finished. I mean, *I'm* going to be in the local paper, and I'm *way* more grounded than her. Oh, well.

"We need something to look forward to," says Amelia. "As a treat to make up for all the trauma."

"What trauma?" I splutter. "It's *normal* to start secondary school."

"Yeah, and it's normal for that to be a *bit* traumatic," says Amelia.

"Yeah," Nat agrees. "This is a very trying time in our lives." The coach starts moving. "Oh my God!"

"I'm excited," I say obstinately.

"I know! Let's get milkshakes at McDonald's afterwards," suggests Amelia.

"Yes!" Nat practically squeals. "We should definitely get milkshakes afterwards."

Oh *great*. My family just blew all our spare money on chocolate biscuits to impress the local press, so there's none left in the kitty for me to get such fripperies. I'll have to be a charity case again. Or not come.

"You'll come, won't you, Jess?" says Nat then.

"Of course," I reply automatically. So charity case it is then. *Urrrgggghhh*. I should be above this now. I'm *famous*. Kind of. But what's the point of being voted to the top of Newsworth if you still can't afford a humble milkshake?

Still, in all fairness, we did buy those biscuits because of me and my cartoon. I suppose I should accept my role in emptying the coffers. I guess you can't win them all.

Our new school is huge. *Huuuuuge*. I cannot

emphasise how big it is. I think it will take me the minimum of a month to find my way around it. I am definitely going to get lost here.

It's so big because it absorbs most of the children from all the local primary schools. I mean, not *everyone*, but probably the majority.

I think nearly all of *our* Year Six are coming here, with just a handful of people going off to different places. We're the nearest school to it, actually. We even have the same name. We're Hillfern Juniors and this school is Hillfern Seniors.

I've been here before on the open day a while ago. I remember being really impressed with the art block and the science labs. There are Bunsen burners and test tubes, and we'll get to do actual *experiments*. How cool is that? I hope we have science as one of our practice lessons today.

We're not doing science. Or art. We spend nearly two hours in a lesson calling itself PSHCE, which apparently stands for "Personal, Social, Health, Career and Economic Education" but seems like a bit of a doss.

We got divided into groups with all the different schools mixed up. I'm in the same class-group as Natalie and Amelia, but I end up sitting next to a girl from St Mary's called Keshma. Keshma is really nice and it turns out we both have little brothers who are sometimes annoying.

To be fair, PSHCE is kind of interesting. Our teacher, Miss Jacobs, is lovely and wants to encourage us to discuss various issues and get to know each other. She says she really wants to make us *think*. It feels a bit weird being asked what our opinions are for once, but I like it.

Then, after morning break – which is *amazing* by the way; there's a canteen where you can get crisps

and iced buns and everything – we
go back into our PSHCE lesson
for a balloon debate.

The title "balloon debate" is misleading. I
thought we were going to have a discussion about
whether balloons are good for the
environment or something. But
it turns out we had to pretend a
whole bunch of famous people
were in a hot-air balloon
that's sinking fast, and they'll
all die unless one person is
chucked out. *Harsh.*

We had to get into pairs (I
went with Keshma) and each
pair was given a famous person
to defend, and say why he or she
shouldn't be chucked out of the balloon.

Keshma and I worked really well as a team. We
came up with loads of great reasons why our person,
Florence Nightingale, should survive. The best of
these was how useful her medical skills would be in
the event of a crash-landing. She totally made it as a
survivor, thanks to us. Result.

"I *love* it here," I proclaim to Natalie and Amelia at lunchtime, as we were walking aimlessly around the grounds, finishing our ice lollies. (*Ice lollies*, thank you very much! This school sells them for 20p! Even *I* can afford ice lollies!)

"I wouldn't go that far," says Amelia.

Amelia and Natalie had to be Steve Collins, the unpopular *X Factor* judge, in the balloon debate. He was kind of hard to defend. They only survived being chucked out because another team had to be boy band MBlaze, and it turns out our new class collectively *really* hates MBlaze.

"Don't worry about the balloon debate," I tell them.

"I'm not, thanks," says Amelia defensively. "Hopefully we can have some *proper* lessons, that actually *matter*, this afternoon."

It is at this point that some older boys run past, shouting, "Stupid Year Sevens!"

Natalie looks absolutely shocked. "Do you think they were talking to *us*?"

Well, yes, obviously, I think. But I decide to make

light of it. "Well, no, because *technically* we're not in Year Seven, so they can't have been."

"They were," sighs Amelia. "This school is full of brutes and idiots."

"And ice lollies," I add. "That's not a *terrible* trade-off."

"It is," says Natalie, looking worried.

Natalie and Amelia seem on edge for the rest of the day, and don't perk up again until we're in McDonald's. And that's when I perk down a bit because I'm embarrassed I can't buy my own milkshake. Again.

CHAPTER 12

As I ride the bus to school the next day, I suddenly realise why Natalie and Amelia seemed so bothered by those boys. I can't believe I didn't work it out sooner.

At Hillfern Juniors, Natalie has led quite a charmed life. She's always been popular and cool and pretty and charming, whereas I used to get "stupid chess club" shouted at me sometimes by mean boys.

That all stopped when Tanya started calling me "Toons" and handed out photocopies of my satirical cartoon of our school. Then people stopped calling me names when they were bored and I became a kind of cool(ish) oddball.

But on the inside, I still expect to get shouted at a bit. That just seems normal. And it doesn't bother me that much. A *bit*, obviously. But it doesn't ruin my day. I guess I'm just more used to the idea that not everyone will like you. I can be quite good at ignoring it (sometimes) or sticking up for myself (sometimes). You have to take the rough with the smooth.

But Nat and Amelia, they've always been top dogs, so they've never had to learn those skills. And there'll be a whole new pecking order at secondary school, with Year Sevens right at the bottom of it.

I sense a weird atmosphere as I take my seat outside the library for the next comic meeting. I wonder if it's because they're intimidated by me now that my article has come out? I should probably find a way to reassure them I'm still the same person I always was. I'm still just like them, mostly.

Because today I am having *my moment*. My fifteen minutes of fame. The interview is in the paper! For all to see. But I'm being really cool about it. Like, I just *casually* held the paper in my hand in the form room before registration, until Natalie noticed and said, "Oooh! Let's see then!"

But the point is, no one can say I was *going on about it*. I was merely providing *visual clues* so that other people could discover the wonder of me for themselves.

The paper used two photos in the end. A close-up of me holding my cartoon picture, and one with Ryan and Lady and me sitting on the floor drawing eerily dismembered Homer Simpson heads.

I'm not sure how to break the silence, and then Lewis says casually, "I read the article."

"Oh cool, you got a copy!" I smile broadly, to show how normal I still am. "What did you think?"

They all exchange looks with each other, for

slightly too long. Surely they can't find me *that* intimidating now?

"Well," says Joshua finally, "I think it's cool. The pictures are fun, and you come across well."

"Thanks," I say. Why does he seem so reserved, though?

"I think *it doesn't mention the comic*," says Lewis.

"*What?*" I am genuinely surprised. I mean, I read the article this morning, but I wasn't *thinking* about the comic then. "That can't be right. I mentioned the comic *loads*. I swear I did."

Tanya gets out the paper and I scan the interview. "Local Girl is Top of the Spots," says the headline, with a line underneath explaining, "Viral Hit For Eleven-Year-Old Cartoonist." Then there's a quote from me in bold, saying, "**My hero is Matt Groening.**" But Lewis is right, none of the article mentions the comic.

"Guys, I really did talk about it," I say earnestly and yet somehow sounding guilty. "I really did. But I kept being interrupted. My dad kept coming in with tea, and my brother kept trying to make the dog do tricks it doesn't do, and it was really hard to get them to listen. The journalist seemed more interested in how good my Homer Simpson heads were. She kept asking me if I wanted to be an animator at Disney."

"You should have tried harder," says Lewis haughtily.

"I *did* try hard!" I start to feel annoyed. "I said I don't want to be an animator at Disney, I want my comic to take off, but she didn't put that in."

"Well, it says here you're *considering* a career at Disney," supplies Tanya.

"When have you *ever* heard me mention Disney?" I splutter. "It's not *my* fault if she changed what I said."

That blimmin' Pamela-the-journalist. Eating all our chocolate biscuits and misquoting me. Thanks for *nothing*.

"You sold us out," says Lewis suddenly. "You're a sell-out."

What? How *dare* he?

WHAT??!

"I did *everything* you asked for. Do you want me to get the recording of the interview from the paper? I can prove it to you." Then I lose my temper. "It's not my fault if they think *I'm* more interesting than the comic. I tried my best. You *could* still thank me for trying instead of having a go at me."

"Well," says Lewis coldly. "It still looks to me like you walked all over us to get your place in the limelight."

What the −? "Well, Lewis," I reply hotly, "maybe when *you've* had a cartoon go to the top of Newsworth, you can talk to me about *limelight*."

There's a pause while they all look at each other. Finally Tanya sighs and breaks the silence. "Look, it's all right, Toons, I'm sure you did your best. But this just goes to show, it's tough out there. Maybe one of us should come with you next time."

"*Next time?*" Am I seeing *anger stars*? (Is that a thing?)

"If you're not up to the job, we can help. We're a team, after all."

"*Not up to the job?* Are you *kidding* me?" I'm outraged.

"You don't need to get angry," says Tanya matter-of-factly. (But I *am* angry.) "Everyone is good at different things."

"Yeah, and you're just not very good at interviews," chips in Lewis.

Now I am *livid. Lewis* is lecturing LIVID

me on interviews? The boy who barely *speaks ever* is telling me I did a bad job at *talking*? This is the *living end*.

And I'd *love* to see them try and do a *better* job. *As if* they could have come round my house and pompously kept us *on-message* with my mad family running about. They would have ended up trying to convince the dog to sit up for a biscuit at the first opportunity.

It's all very well telling me what to do *in theory*, but they have no idea how tough it is at the front line of the publicity machine. I hope there *is* a next time so they can see it for themselves.

And anyway, why aren't they more *grateful*? I only promised them I'd *try*. Some people would have point-blank refused. That was really benevolent of me. I don't deserve this shabby treatment.

But, annoyed as I am, I do also feel bad. I really did *want* to promote the comic. I still love the comic, and working with them on it. Even if they don't seem to appreciate me.

This must be what they mean when they say fame is a fickle friend. It makes your friends hate you.

CHAPTER 13

"Shut up, Jess, we don't want to hear it any more," says Natalie eventually. "We're *trying* to enjoy our Saturday at the mall."

"But don't you think they're **OUT OF ORDER!** out of order?" I protest. "Especially Lewis."

Things were starting to blow over after the interview, but then the local free paper picked up the story of my viral success, and so did a couple of other minor news outlets. And they just copied bits verbatim from the original interview, so the rest of my comic team kept being freshly outraged that the *Hell*fern comic didn't get a mention.

"*I* do," says Amelia. "Lewis is a total nerd. I don't know why you hang around with him."

"No, it's not that, it's the *hypocrisy* of him," I explain. "As if *he* could have done any better. He's so quiet and shy."

"Yeah, because he's a nerd." Amelia is very fashion-conscious and prejudiced against anyone she sees as uncool, so it's difficult to draw her attention to the actual issue.

"He's so pompous with it," I elaborate. "I mean, the guy really does look down on me. And I've tried really hard to be nice and turn a blind eye, but now he's openly criticising me, I just see red."

"*Nerd*," insists Amelia.

"No, it's *not* that he's a nerd, it's that he's a hypocrite, and doesn't appreciate me, and thinks he's loads better than me." Why can I not get a simple point across?

"That's practically the *definition* of a nerd," says Amelia. "Jessica, just say *Lewis is a bratty nerd.* You'll feel so much better."

"Oh my God, you're both boring me so much!" says Nat crossly. "Jess, you should be happy your story is everywhere. Who cares what the others think? You know you tried your hardest. Just forget about them. OK?"

"Yeah, you're right," I say. "Thanks, Nat." And I really try to let those words seep in and ease my guilt, undoing all the cross words as they go. I *should* be happy with my success. I don't have to let anything spoil it.

We traipse aimlessly around the mall, looking at hats and bracelets and sunglasses cases, and it's quite a lot of fun actually.

We take pictures of each other in funny hats, and pose by the cardboard cut-out of an action hero outside the cinema. Nat pulls a face like he smells and I pretend I'm about to punch him.

Then we manage to take a really funny one of all

three of us with the action hero in the background and Amelia suggests it would be a réally nice idea to get it printed on to key rings, so we go to this little kiosk.

I can just about afford it, which is kind of annoying, as I just got my pocket money and for once I would have been able to buy my own milkshake next time we're in McDonald's, but I don't want to *not* get a key ring with our faces on either.

"This is a really lovely keepsake," says Amelia. "We can remember each other forever."

"Well, every time we use a key anyway," I joke.

"We don't need to remember each other forever," Nat points out. "We're all going to the same school next year anyway."

"Er, yes, sure," says Amelia quickly. But why does she look a tiny bit shifty?

"It will still be a lovely thing to have," says Nat.

"We could get it put on mugs and T-shirts too," I say, looking at the things on display in the kiosk. "Or cushions, or—"

"Yes, we've all got eyes, thanks," says Nat. But I think my eyes are more observant than hers, because I don't think she noticed anything fishy about the way Amelia was talking about keepsakes and future schools. *Hmmm.*

Delighted with our new key rings, Natalie and Amelia decide they want to check out the stationery shop – which I LOVE. It might be my favourite shop ever, so we head over there and try out all the pens on all the little bits of paper.

Most people just do squiggles to see what colour or how thick each pen is, but we like to write funny stuff. We never write anything too rude, but once I wrote "wee" and the woman in the shop frowned at me.

WEE

"Excuse me?" I freeze at the voice behind me. It's her. The shop woman who doesn't like *wee.* (Understandably. I mean, who *does* like wee? But that's not the point.) "Excuse me?" the voice comes again.

I look down at what I've written: "Talk to the hand" with a picture of a hand with an arrow pointing at it. It's not rude.

She can't chuck me out for that. Maybe I'm taking up too much space on the pad?

Please don't chuck me out of my favourite shop, I think, as I turn slowly around. I could offer to buy the pen maybe?

"Hello," says the shop woman as I face her. "Are you the girl from the paper?"

I'm too stunned to respond. "Um," I manage.

"You look really like the girl who drew the funny dolphin cartoon for her sister's charity," explains the woman.

"It *is* her!" Nat has been observing this and, amused, comes to my rescue. She places her hands on my shoulders and pushes me forward a step, snapping me out of my shock.

"I'm Jessica," I say. "I mean, yes, I drew the cartoon of the dolphins, and I was in the paper."

"I'm Bev," smiles the shop lady. She reaches out and we shake hands. "I really enjoyed reading about you. Such a lovely story. Makes a nice change from all the usual doom and gloom."

"Thank you," I say. It starts to sink in that I have been *recognised*. By a *stranger*. I am officially a *better* subject than the *usual doom and gloom*. Which isn't really *much* of a compliment, but still nice to hear.

"I was really impressed that your cartoon went viral too," says the shop lady. *Bev*. "You're obviously talented."

"Thank you," I say again.

Bev hesitates. "I don't suppose, um, by any chance, that you bought the pen you drew it with at this shop? I've seen you in here a few times."

I think *wee* and blush. "Um, well, yes," I say. "I mean, it was a birthday present, but it was from here."

"In that case, would you – and stop me if you're in a hurry," says Bev, "but would you mind if I took your photo? It might be something we could use as a bit of an advert for the shop."

"Um…"

"Nothing too fancy or demanding," she adds hastily. "I was just thinking that perhaps I could put it up with a sign saying 'Pen & Ink, as visited by famous local cartoonist' or something. I think you could make our store look more highbrow and appealing."

She obviously doesn't remember about the wee after all!

"Well…" I look at Nat and Amelia, and sort of grin awkwardly. Nat smiles and Amelia shrugs.

"I'll give you some free pens for your trouble…" offers Bev, looking hopefully at me.

"I'll do it!" I say.

The next few minutes go by in a blur, as Bev takes photos of me holding various bits of stationery in various locations of the shop. Nat and Amelia loiter by the door and look bored.

"I think we're nearly done," says Bev.

"Nearly done!" I call out to Natalie and Amelia, trying not to grin too much.

It really feels like I'm a celebrity now. I mean, look, I can't even walk down the *street* without people wanting my photograph. Kind of. This is *amazing*.

"Thanks ever so much," says Bev. "Choose anything you like from the displays. Go nuts."

"Wow, thanks," I say. "Can my friends choose some stuff too?"

"Yes, I don't see why not."

Bev presents me with a huge pack of colouring pens and a pad, and insists I take them. I take a couple of the pens we tested, and a calligraphy pen that looks exciting. But then I feel like that's enough and I don't want to be too cheeky. Natalie chooses a gold and a silver pen, and Amelia chooses a purple pen with a pink fluffy thing on the end of it.

I *love* stationery. I *love* this. This has been such a great day.

"How cool was *that*?" I say as the three of us head off to get the bus home.

"Very cool," says Nat obligingly.

"I'm glad I was able to get pens for you guys too," I say. "At least it makes up for some of the milkshakes."

"Yes, thanks," says Amelia.

"This is great, isn't it?" I say again. I still can't believe that just happened.

"It is," says Natalie, and smiles at me, but I'm

pretty sure I see her and Amelia roll their eyes. I guess being the object of everyone's jealousy is just something I'll have to get used to now.

CHAPTER 14

"Tammy, I don't see what the problem is," I say, bewildered.

"I'm gobsmacked at your betrayal!" says Tammy angrily.

"There's no need to shout." My dad is trying (and failing) to placate my sister. The kitchen has become a courtroom, and Tammy is prosecutor, judge and jury all rolled into one.

"I can't *believe* how quickly you sold out," says Tammy scathingly.

"What are you talking about?" I cry. "Can't you help the environment and still like pens?"

"No, you can't *claim* to like the environment and then move into advertising," argues Tammy. "It's hypocritical. Big business is part of the problem we're fighting against."

"But Pen & Ink is a *small* business," I explain. "That's why Bev paid me in pens."

"Well, I hope you enjoyed your twenty pieces of silver!" says Tammy dramatically.

"Thirty," says Dad.

"What?" says Tammy.

"Judas betrayed Jesus for *thirty* pieces of silver, not twenty. If that's what you're on about."

Honestly, whose side is he on? I didn't betray *anyone*. I don't think. Certainly not on purpose anyway.

"Does it matter?" asks Tammy.

"What's all this noise?" My mum enters the kitchen through the back door carrying food shopping. "I can hear you outside."

"Accuracy always matters," mumbles my dad. Then, more brightly, "Anyone for a cup of tea?"

"Yes, please," says Mum.

"No pieces of silver changed hands," I say. "It was

really more of a favour if anything."

"Have *you* heard about this?" Tammy demands of Mum. "Your middle child is selling her soul. She's *advertising*."

"I have heard about it," says Mum, starting to unpack the shopping. "And I do think you were a bit foolish, Jessica," she tells me.

"*Thank you*," says Tammy smugly.

"Really?" I ask Mum.

"Yes," says Mum. "You didn't even try to negotiate. You should have spoken to me or your dad. Never accept a first offer."

"What!" cries Tammy, outraged. "I'm not complaining that she didn't get *adequately remunerated* for her endorsement. I'm saying she shouldn't have done it *at all*."

"Oh, right," says Mum.

I hate fighting with Tammy. It doesn't happen very often and I'm suddenly worried I might cry. I don't know if Tammy notices my face change, but she suddenly says, "Look, Jess, I'm not having a go at you." Which nearly makes me burst into hysterical laughter.

"Well, you could have fooled me," I mutter.

"Look, it's just..." Tammy pauses, evidently thinking carefully about what to say. "I'm against the entire ethos of advertising. And it's important for you to think through how what seem like small decisions you make on the spur of the moment can impact on lots of other, bigger, things."

She takes a deep breath. "I'm sorry if I yelled at you. I just felt so disappointed at the idea of you using your talent to go against everything I believe in. But I know you didn't do it on purpose. And ultimately it's up to you what you do."

"OK," I say, still a bit confused. I mean, I hadn't completely thought of it like that before.

"But please don't grow up and go and work in advertising," Tammy adds.

"Unless it's advertising for charities," says Dad jovially.

Honestly, the modern world is a *minefield*. So it's OK to advertise a good cause but not stationery. But I think stationery *is* a good cause. I really like stationery.

"Is that why you came over here, Tammy?" asks Mum, putting shopping haphazardly away. "To rain on Jessica's parade?"

"What? No, and I've just *apologised* to Jessica," says Tammy indignantly.

Huh, has she? Well, I suppose she *sort of* has. I guess I'll take it.

"Just come to spend a nice family Sunday with us then, have you?" asks Dad, chuckling.

"Good one," chuckles Mum, as Dad hands her a cup of tea.

"No, actually I've come to tell Mum about developments with her food blog," says Tammy.

"Oh yes?" Mum sits at the table with her tea and Tammy sits down opposite her. "I've been looking at the stats, the way you showed me," says Mum. "They're going up all the time."

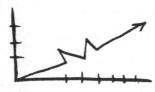

"Yes, it's going really well," agrees Tammy. "Just like I said it would."

"I've been updating it with more recipes, and

replying to comments and questions," says Mum. "There's been quite a lot of them too, actually."

"Well, that's what I wanted to ask you about," says Tammy. "Would you be interested in giving a talk?"

"What kind of talk?" says Dad. "Your mother isn't into rabble-rousing, as you well know."

"Says Tree Man!" I can't help but refer to Dad's time as an activist.

"Don't be cheeky, Jessica," says Mum. "Yes, what kind of talk?" she asks Tammy.

"It's a support group for single parents and low-income families," says Tammy. "At the community centre. There'll be other speakers as well. You'll just have to talk for fifteen to twenty minutes about cooking and eating healthily on a reduced budget."

"Is that not a bit … patronising?" asks Mum carefully.

"Well, it might be if you hadn't lived through it yourself," says Tammy. "Believe me, people want to know this stuff. You must have noticed you get the same questions coming up again and again on the blog?" Mum nods. "Well, you're just going to answer those questions all at once to a room full of people."

"So it'll be a Q and A session?" asks Dad, enjoying bringing some management-speak into the conversation.

"At the end," says Tammy. "If you could just condense your best tips, your cheapest or easiest meals, and chat about those for ten minutes, then we'll open it up to the floor for questions. I've been to these things before, Mum. They're nice, honestly."

"Hmmm," says Mum. "I'm not sure."

"You can do it," I say to her encouragingly. "You can teach a room full of strangers how to eat gone-off kidney beans."

"There was nothing wrong with those kidney beans, Jessica," says Mum huffily. "I sniffed them and they were fine. None of us got sick, did we?"

"That's the spirit," I say.

"I don't think that's the kind of thing they want to hear," says Dad.

"Actually it is," says Tammy. "That will make everyone feel loads better about themselves. Definitely mention any disasters too. That'll be funny and break the ice."

"I can write you a list if you like?" I offer.

Mum laughs and tells me I'm cheeky. Then she

affectionately ruffles my hair. "OK, I'll do it." She really is in a good mood these days.

"Let me know if you need any tips on public speaking and the fame game," I tell her. "I'm a dab hand these days."

Later, as I'm helping Mum put the bins out, we bump into our next-door neighbours, the VanDerks, tidying their front lawn. I'm worried this will seriously impact on my mum's good mood.

"Hello there!" Mr VanDerk waves and turns off his leaf blower.

"Get ready for a lot of hot air!" Mum says to me, just as the noise of the machine cuts out. I fight a mad urge to giggle.

"Sorry?" says Mr VanDerk, frowning.

"Your leaf blower," explains Mum. "It must be full of hot air."

"Well, no," says Mr VanDerk. "It's cold air, actually."

Mum and I laugh. I love this happy side of my mum. She's carefree and cheeky, and doesn't care

126

what the neighbours think. She's basically Auntie Joan. I can see how they're sisters now. (Other than because they both like shouting so much.)

"So how's things?" Mum asks obligingly, as both VanDerks step over to us.

"Oh, very good, thanks," says  Mrs VanDerk. "I've been baking cakes to help raise money for the Anti-Graffiti League. They've been going down a treat. Of course, none of them are *green*."

Both VanDerks look at me and chortle. *Honestly.* My green-cake fiasco was *two years* ago. Move on, people. I'm an Internet sensation now. Please react accordingly.

"Yep," smiles Mr VanDerk, putting his arm around his wife. "She's *quite* the domestic goddess," he simpers.

"How lovely," says Mum. "Me too!"

"Sorry?" Both VanDerks look a bit cross.

"I've become a bit of a domestic goddess myself," explains Mum. "I've got my own website  with recipes I invented. And people seem to be going nuts for them."

"*You?*" Mrs VanDerk can't quite seem to hide her disdain.

"That's right." Mum nods. "I'm doing a talk about it soon at the community centre."

"How *extraordinary*," says Mr VanDerk.

"*You?*" repeats Mrs VanDerk, apparently discombobulated by this turn of events. Mum nods again, smiling.

I notice Mum has neglected to mention the *budget* angle of her new-found cooking fame and success. It definitely sounds more glamorous that way, more *domestic goddess-y*. But then she blows it.

"Well, must be getting on," says Mum. "Those soya chunks aren't going to soak *themselves* in lightly salted water."

The VanDerks both pull slightly disgusted faces as they are forced to picture our dinner.

"Cheerio," manages Mrs VanDerk.

"What a world," says Mr VanDerk.

CHAPTER 15

"Good news, everyone!" I greet Joshua, Tanya and Lewis by the comfy chairs in the Quiet Reading Area as usual.

"Oh yes?" says Tanya.

"Um, hang on, shouldn't we finish what we were talking about before Jessica interrupts?" says Lewis. He *definitely* dislikes me more than he used to. But I think the feeling is probably mutual.

"Nah." Tanya waves a dismissive hand at Lewis. "If Toons says she has good news, I wanna hear it now." I knew there was a reason Tanya is a great friend. Stuff like this.

"OK." I sit down, nodding my thanks to Tanya. "I've been invited to be part of an event at the comic shop in our town. Which means *we've* been invited. Let's plan a strategy to launch the comic there!"

"Oh my *God*!" Tanya actually hugs me. And she's *really* not a *hugs* kind of girl. She must be super-pleased about this. I *knew* she would be.

"Whoa!" Joshua is impressed. "You've been invited to take part in *this*?" He pulls a leaflet out of his school bag. It has "Comic-tacular" written on it in comic-type lettering.

"Yeah, cool," I say. "You already know about it?"

"Of course I do," says Joshua. "I'm a regular at Big Dave's comic shop."

"Excellent," says Tanya. "You're our man on the inside. What's the lie of the land?"

"Big Dave hates children," says Joshua. "He blanks anyone who even *looks* under the age of twelve. He just won't answer your questions. Sometimes he points by way of an answer. I think he's been forced to start staging kid-friendly events because of the recession. He won't be happy about it."

"Interesting," says Tanya. "Let's see this leaflet. Who else is going to be there?"

"Some quite good people, actually," says Joshua. "Big Dave does know everyone. They'll definitely be queuing to get this guy's autograph." Joshua points at a name on the leaflet as he hands it to Tanya.

"I can't see you in this, Toons?" Tanya studies the leaflet, turning it over.

"I'm *other guests yet to be announced*," I say. "Someone called Miriam, who is helping Big Dave, said they want to do a quick interview with me about why I like drawing cartoons, how I got into it and what it was like to go viral."

"I wonder why they booked you?" says Lewis.

"Excuse me?" I say. Did I not literally just explain this?

"Well, I mean, you just drew a dolphin. It's not like you're a big comic person."

"*Two* dolphins," I correct him. "Talking to each other with a speech bubble."

"And she *is* a big comic person," corrects Tanya. "We're launching *our comic*, you daft wally."

"And," I add, "Miriam said it's because lots of the kids who buy comics want to draw comics too, and it might be nice for them to hear from someone successful near their own age." Do I sound a bit haughty? Hmmm.

"Anyway," says Joshua, clearly thinking I do. "We need to think about how we do this."

"I have an idea," I say.

"All ears, Toons," says Tanya. "You've got the floor."

"OK," I say. "At the moment our comic is – understandably – very school-focused."

"Obviously," says Lewis.

"So if we were to try to, for example, sell it in a comic shop, most people wouldn't get half the references."

"True," agrees Joshua.

"My solution to this problem," I reveal, "is we should make a *best of*."

"A best of?" asks Lewis, screwing his face up unnecessarily.

I ignore him. "We've got loads of brilliant jokes and comic strips that don't mention the school at all. We should make a compilation of the very best ones, like a calling card. It will be our sales pitch and our product in one. A *best of*."

"That is *brilliant*, Toons," says Tanya, clapping me on the back and making me cough.

"It's a really good idea," agrees Joshua.

"Hmmmm," says Lewis thoughtfully, though he can't seem to find fault with it.

"Right," says Joshua. "So what goes in?"

"Definitely Roland the slightly rubbish superhero," says Lewis. "That doesn't mention school at all."

"Good call," agrees Tanya.

"We'll have to decide on two or three of the best Rolands," I say. They nod.

"Jess, that cartoon you did of the bee and the wasp having an argument is perfect," says Joshua.

"Definitely," agrees Tanya.

"Yeah, it is actually," says Lewis.

And just like that, somehow we are all partaking in *teamwork*. Phew.

After a lengthy debate, we agree on two Roland strips, my cartoon about the bee and the wasp, and various other bits and pieces that best represent what we can do, giving all the different *flavours*. Now all we need to do is get them arranged on the pages and printed nicely.

Oh my God, *oh my God*, I'm about to **OMG** step out in front of an audience in the comic shop and talk about cartoons! Oh my God. It's going to be fine. It's definitely going to be fine. Definitely.

"Please welcome Jessica Morris!" I hear Miriam's voice, and step out from behind the little curtain to polite applause.

This is *phase one* of the cunning plan that Tanya has put together. I'm not completely sure about it. Though, to be fair, *phase two* is where things get scary.

Phase one is simple: Miriam interviews me for five minutes and I try to mention the comic as much as possible. I've been coached on this by Tanya, and I just have to "not take no for an answer" when trying to crowbar in the comic.

Then, once I've brilliantly set the scene with constant comic references, comes phase two. Joshua, Tanya and Lewis will burst out surprisingly and reveal that our comic is available to buy NOW! And at such low, low prices.

Like I said, I'm not sure about it.

I sit on the stool opposite Miriam. There's a picture of my dolphin cartoon blown up on a projector screen behind us.

"So, Jessica, thank you for being here with us today," says Miriam. "How did it feel when your cartoon got shared by thousands of people on the Internet and went viral?"

"Amazing," I say. "Nearly as amazing as the feeling of when I launched my own comic with some friends at school." Miriam nods. Tanya gives me a thumbs up from the audience.

"Wonderful. And what made you decide to draw the cartoon? Is the environment something close to your heart? Have you been inspired by reading *Captain Planet* comics? Or

Aquaman protecting the sea? Or even Swamp Thing defending the forests?"

There are some chuckles from the audience at these references.

"Um, kind of," I say. "It was my sister who wanted me to draw it. She's an activist. But I do care about global warming as well, and we are probably the last generation that can do anything about it."

I glance across the room and catch Tanya's eye. She gestures with her hand for me to keep talking, so I add, "But normally I draw funny cartoons about my school, with my friends that I run my comic with."

Miriam ignores this. "And how do you sit down to draw a cartoon?"

"Well, if it's for my comic, sometimes we all sit down together and brainstorm ideas—"

"No," Miriam interrupts. "How do *you* come up with ideas? We don't want to hear about your friends. *You're* the star here today."

"Oh, um." I can't help but feel

flattered. I'm the *star* here today. I mean, we all heard the lady. And at least Tanya and the others are here to witness first-hand how difficult it can be to keep talking about something if people aren't interested in it.

And did I mention, I'm the *star*? I can't let my public down. The people need answers. I launch into an explanation about how I sit at my desk thinking, and kind of let my brain go into free fall by asking myself questions about what certain ideas might look like.

"That's very interesting," proclaims Miriam. "That will probably be very useful for anyone here today who has ever struggled to come up with new ideas." We both look at the audience. Some of them are nodding. Wow, I'm *interesting*. To upwards of three people. But still, three people!

We carry on chatting for a bit longer, and I make a couple more half-hearted attempts to crowbar in the comic, but to be honest, I'm sort of enjoying talking about *myself*.

As we get towards the end of our conversation,

I catch Tanya's frantic face, so I ask if I can add something, and Miriam says yes.

"As a special exclusive to Comic-tacular, I'd like to announce the launch of the *Hell*fern comic! Ta da!"

At this, Joshua and Lewis appear from nowhere, holding a small stack of the new *best of* edition.

"At low, low prices!" I add, trying not to look at Miriam. "A special introductory rate."

Miriam stares at me incredulously then says to the audience, "OK, we're going to take a short break now."

As soon as the mics are off and everyone is milling around not paying attention to us, Miriam addresses me irritably. "What was that?"

"Um, my comic?" I offer.

"You should have run that by me," says Miriam crossly. "Everything like that has to be approved."

"Sorry," I say, feeling immediately awful and small, after feeling so big when everyone was impressed by my words.

"It's very unprofessional," she adds. "Why didn't you tell me you wanted to do that?"

"*Hello there*, the name's Tanya Harris!" Suddenly Tanya is by my side, brashly offering her hand to be shaken by Miriam, who hesitates, then does shake it.

"Hello," says Miriam, still sounding cross.

"I'm afraid that was my bad, Mrs M," says Tanya. "I thought it would be a nice surprise."

"Well, it wasn't, and my name is Miriam. Please don't call me Mrs M."

"Right you are," says Tanya happily. "Well, you can't blame a kid for trying."

"Well, you can, actually," says Miriam. "I've got a schedule to stick to and I need to know what's going on in order to keep on top of things. The whole thing falls apart if people start introducing amateurish theatrics."

"As I say, it's my bad, and it won't happen again," says Tanya, unrepentant. "I take full responsibility. But you know, one person's *amateurish theatrics* is another person's *enterprising*. We all have to start somewhere."

"I suppose." Miriam sighs and looks at Tanya with what could be a grudging respect. "So," she says finally. "You're a new venture that wants to join the world of capitalist enterprise, are you?"

"Absolutely we are, yes," says Tanya.

"All right then," says Miriam. "You can sell your comic in here *just this once*. But we get a twenty per cent cut of anything you make."

"Normally I would not accept a first offer," says Tanya, somehow with a completely straight face. "But I can see you're a busy woman, and I'd like to make amends, so you've got yourself a deal." They shake hands again.

"Great," says Miriam drily. "Well, I need to prep the next speaker. Nice interview, Jessica." And with that she's gone.

I turn to Tanya with renewed awe. "Am I the best or am I the best?" she asks, grinning.

"That was some mighty fine negotiating," I tell her honestly. Tanya is *brilliant* at solving problems – which admittedly she has also created – but *still*. I am definitely impressed.

And that event definitely went brilliantly, for me and the comic. High fives all round.

CHAPTER 16

"*Someone's* in the paper again!" Dad throws the local paper over to me. I look at the page he means and see a little article with the headline: "Local cartoonist makes splash at comic event." There's a picture of me talking to Miriam, and you can see some of the audience's heads and my dolphin cartoon in the background on the screen.

Wow, I didn't know there'd be *press* there. I don't remember any photos being taken. I read on. It's a summary of some of the things I said in my interview. *Cool.*

CooL

"Don't get too big-headed," warns Mum, looking up from the family laptop (where she has been tracking her Web page hits again).

The phone rings. Ryan leaps to answer it and then hands it to Mum. "It's sort of for you."

"Sort of?" Mum takes the phone and listens to the other person with a bemused look on her face. "Right, yes, OK. Thank you. We'll have to get back to you on that." She hangs up and looks at me. "Well, Jessica, opportunity knocks again!"

Oh my God, oh my God. *I've been asked to draw a comic strip for the local paper!* It's a dream come true! *Talk about a legacy.* Not that I care about that any more, obviously. I'm just saying. And anyway, I didn't *start* that whole legacy business.

Apparently the journalist who was at the Comictacular event bought one of our comics! (We actually sold five in total, how amazing is that? We sold them for 20p each, so made one pound in total, but we had to give twenty per cent to Miriam, which was 20p, so we walked away with a cool 80p. Which I know isn't really very much, but as Tanya kept repeating, you do have to start somewhere. And I could totally buy an ice lolly at my new school with my share, so I feel like a winner.)

$20p \times 5 - 20\% = 80p$

143

Anyway, the journalist especially liked the cartoon I drew of the bee dressed as a wasp at the bee fancy-dress party. He showed it to some other people at the paper, and they had a meeting and all agreed it might be fun to give me a trial run, drawing a cartoon for them every week, starting with the bee one. They want to *publish* my bee cartoon *in the paper*! Under *my* name. Like I'm a *real cartoonist*.

This is literally the most amazing thing that has ever happened to me. I've *arrived*. I have landed my dream job at the age of eleven. And it really is a job, too. I am going to be paid twenty pounds per cartoon! Twenty whole pounds!

Mum and Dad are making me put at least half of it into a savings account as a condition of letting me to do it, but still, that's ten whole pounds a week to spend lavishly on McDonald's milkshakes if I so choose. Gone are my days of begging for scraps from the table or a slurp of Natalie's milkshake. No, sir, I've hit the *big time*.

Joshua, Tanya and Lewis took it really well. I was

slightly worried they might be annoyed and say I hadn't bigged up the comic enough, or that Lewis might demand to know where *his* offer of a comic strip was, but they're all still really happy about selling five copies of the comic. And as Tanya said, what makes one of us look good makes all of us look good. And I was really nice and tactful in the way I told them.

Admittedly, I was a bit more overly gleeful when I told Natalie and Amelia, but only because they were so *cartoons-aren't-a-thing* before. I don't think I could have more conclusively proved cartoons *are-actually-a-thing* unless I had made a cartoons T-shirt that said, "We Are Too a Thing" on it.

But, gleefulness aside, success hasn't changed me. It definitely hasn't gone to my head. And when the inevitable TV show is made about my life, I'll totally suggest my comic friends as writers. I mean, if you let someone write or star on your TV show, they should totally just be grateful about it. Right? Ha, I'm mainly kidding.

The best part is, I'm allowed to have a little party in the back garden to celebrate my success. (I have to let Ryan come, though.)

Auntie Joan comes, too, and puts some money towards the food, so my parents decide to have a barbecue! This is seriously the best my life has ever got.

I invite Natalie, Amelia, Joshua, Tanya, Lewis, Emily, Megan, Fatimah, Cherry and Shantair, and then Mum says that's enough. I only really invited Lewis so that Joshua wouldn't be the only boy, but we are still *colleagues* after all.

I feel like I haven't had a party round my house for ages. This is so much fun. It's a lovely sunny day, everyone is excited that school is almost over and everyone seems to be having a good time.

"Ahoy there," says Mr VanDerk, appearing on the other side of the fence.

"Hello!" Dad waves back jovially through the

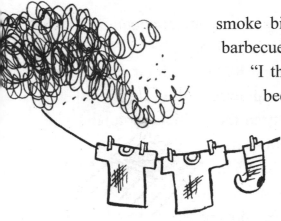

smoke billowing from the barbecue.

"I think it might have been nice of you to *warn* us you were going to have a barbecue," says Mr VanDerk. "That smoke is going all over our clean washing."

"Yes, it's the wind," explains Dad.

"Well, I rather think it's the smoke, actually," says Mr VanDerk.

Auntie Joan stops playing catch with Ryan, to better listen to their conversation.

"Oh well," says Dad cheerfully. "Can't be helped."

"That's very inconsiderate," says Mr VanDerk.

"Is it?" asks Auntie Joan, stepping towards Mr VanDerk. "I seem to remember you had a barbecue the last time I was here, and I don't think you tipped *us* off about our washing."

Mr VanDerk looks flustered at being challenged. "Well, I hardly think a tit-for-tat attitude is helpful. And anyway the smoke blows *away* from your side."

"I'm not sure you understand how *wind* works," says Auntie Joan flatly.

Natalie, Amelia and I catch each other's eyes. Is this going to turn into a big fight in front of all my friends? But at that moment my mum comes out with a tray of home-made burgers.

"Here we go! Ready for the barbecue. My own special recipe!" She surveys the Joan and Mr VanDerk stand-off and strides over to them. "Hello there. Would you like to find out for yourself why I have the third-most-successful food blog in the county?" (I can't believe she knows statistics like that. Talk about a big head.)

"No, thank you," replies Mr VanDerk curtly.

"Would you like to try one, Harriet?" Mum calls over to where she's sitting on a cushion under a tree reading a book in Mandarin. She's not far from where Nat, Amelia and I are standing but I hadn't noticed her there.

"No, thank you," Harriet replies without looking up. Then under her breath, "I don't want to get food poisoning."

"OK then!" Mum calls back. "More for us. Joan, give me a hand with these, will you?" And then Mum skilfully leads Joan away from the VanDerks and defuses the conflict.

"We heard what you just said," Amelia tells Harriet.

"I can't help it if I have high standards," says Harriet loftily.

"Shame those high standards don't extend to your clothes," sneers Amelia.

Natalie giggles. I sigh. It would be easier to back Amelia up if she didn't have a go at Harriet for (what I, at least, consider to be) the wrong reasons.

"I have better things to care about," replies Harriet. "Clothes are nearly as dull as the inane conversation you were just having."

"Why were you eavesdropping on us then? If we're so dull?" asks Nat. We were only talking about the end-of-school disco but still, it's not nice to know someone's been sneakily listening in on you.

"I'm actually *trying* to get some peace and quiet, if you don't mind," says Harriet pompously.

149

"It's hardly *my* fault I live next door to a family of chimps and their idiot friends."

I just manage to control myself. "Ignore Harriet, guys," I say calmly. "She's just trying to get a reaction and spoil my party."

But Amelia hates backing down or feeling like she's been in any way bested. And Harriet seems pretty determined to have a fight. She's being much ruder from the safety of her garden than she ever is at school.

"Oh, is *that* what this is?" says Harriet sarcastically. "A *party*? I thought it was a scene from *Planet of the Apes*." Sticking with the monkey theme then. The joke's on *her*; I really *like* monkeys.

"Yes, we're celebrating Jessica's *artistic success*,"

boasts Amelia, who is actually probably the least impressed by my cartooning skills out of all my friends, but I guess it's a chance to goad Harriet. "But I suppose you wouldn't know much about that, would you?"

"No, I tend to avoid doodles that *sheep* on the Internet think are good," agrees Harriet disdainfully.

"Yeah, it's so great," continues Amelia. "Jess has been given her own comic strip in the local paper. So awesome for her to have her great talent recognised like that. First she designs brilliant sets for the musical, and now this. She's definitely the best artist in our school."

"*What?*" Harriet stands up, annoyed. "No way. *No way* has Jessica got her own cartoon comic strip in the paper."

"'Fraid so," I say.

I feel slightly awkward because Amelia only brings up my art stuff because she knows it bothers Harriet where slights about fashion and stuff won't. I don't want to be used as bait, but now I'm kind of going along with this.

"You're lying! You're not talented enough," protests Harriet.

Then again, if Harriet wants a battle, she should prepare to lose.

"Well, some people think differently," I reply. "And my pay cheque proves it."

"They're *paying* you?" gasps Harriet.

"Yep. Real money," I state happily. "Some kids get a paper round to make extra cash; I just write for them."

OK, I don't know why I added that last bit. It was a bit smug and undignified, but *still*. Harriet started it. Even if Amelia was the one to make it go nuclear.

"*Unbelievable*," says Harriet, and stomps off into her house, slamming the back door.

CHAPTER 17

"Hey, guys, can I get you a milkshake?" I ask, feeling flush in McDonald's after school.

"Won't that wipe out most of your money?" asks Nat.

Yes, I realise. "No," I lie. "I'm rich now. Rich, I tells you. Sit down, I'll bring them over." I am no longer a charity case, that's the main thing.

I pull the local paper out of my bag while I wait in the queue and admire my handiwork. My wasp and bee cartoon looks totally professional in black and white. This is *awesome*.

"Ah, this is the life!" I sit down at the table with

our milkshakes a moment later and sigh contentedly.

"Uh, Jess, you should maybe look at this," says Natalie, reading something on her phone.

"What?" I ask. She holds her phone out.

"It's sort of about you and your dolphin cartoon."

I take the phone and zoom in. On the screen is a picture of my cartoon – and a picture of another dolphin cartoon, which looks, well, identical. But the other dolphin cartoon is an advert for home insurance. Under the home insurance ad, a caption says, "Insure your home against fire, theft and floods."

I scroll back up the page and see the title of the article is "Did Eleven-Year-Old Steal Insurance Ad?" *Uh-oh*. That's not good. **Uh-oh**

"Is this…?" I stammer. "Are they…?"

"They're saying you copied it, yes," says Nat.

"Noooooo!" I wail. "But I didn't." This is *definitely* not good.

"Well, *you* know you didn't copy it," **NOT GOOD** says Nat. "So that's all that matters, really."

It turns out that *isn't* all that matters at all.

When I get home, Dad tells me the paper have rung and dropped my weekly cartoon. He said they sounded quite annoyed. They're even going to run a story on how disappointed they are in me in the next edition.

"But I didn't steal it!" I tell him.

"Don't worry," says Dad. "I'm sure it will all blow over."

But *will* it all blow over? And even if it does, will my new job blow back to me?

It seems everything has got pretty serious pretty quickly. It's spiralling out of control. And no one seems to be interested in my side of the story.

Apparently the "story" has been picked up by various blogs, and there is general Internet chatter about how the youth of today can't be trusted.

On top of *that*, a trip to the mall shows that my picture in the stationery shop has been taken down. I can't bring myself to go inside, I'm too sad. Plus, I'm worried Bev might want her pens back and I've used some of them.

As what might eventually be known as the Dolphin Fiasco gets worse, school gets worse, too.

Everyone knows about it, and I feel like they're whispering and staring at me, even when they're not.

At least my friends have been really supportive. Joshua said he knew I was innocent because the cartoon is totally my style. Tanya said she was going to start a petition to clear my name, and even Lewis didn't complain I'd brought the precious comic under disrepute.

"Let's go to McDonald's after school again," says Nat. "Get milkshakes and cheer you up."

My heart sinks as the financial implications of this slap me in the face. I am forced to remember that I briefly had some money, and then relive how I lost it again. *Uuurrrggghhh.*

"Thanks, but I might just go home," I say sullenly.

"Don't let it get to you," says Amelia.

"Yeah, it could happen to anyone," says Nat.

Could it?

"But it's so unfair," I sigh. "I didn't steal it."

Out of the corner of my eye I catch Natalie and Amelia exchanging a slight look, and I'm so fragile and paranoid that I call them on it.

"What?" I ask. "What was that look about?"

"Well, it's just…" says Natalie. She glances at Amelia again and then looks guiltily back at me.

"What?" I demand.

"I'm not saying you did it on purpose," she adds quickly, "but you know, maybe you *subconsciously* copied it somehow. You know, without realising it."

"Yeah," continues Amelia. "Maybe you saw it somewhere online, and then forgot that you saw it, and then your subconscious made you draw it."

"That *isn't* what happened," I say incredulously.

"You don't know that for sure though, do you?" says Nat. "Your brain *could* have tricked you."

"It is a *bit* suspicious otherwise," says Amelia. "The cartoons are very similar."

"Thanks!" I say sarcastically. "Are you trying to make me think I'm going mad?"

I *hate* everyone mistrusting me like this. This is so horrible. I can't believe how badly things have gone.

I was *so* looking forward to school ending on a brilliant high, but now I'll be leaving under a cloud of shame. And everyone will remember me as the girl who *stole a cartoon*. I sigh inwardly.

Still, what a legacy, eh? I'm kind of notorious. Like a Guy Fawkes or something. Part of me can't help but be darkly amused that I have at least cracked that. And at least things can't get any worse.

"Well, well, well," says Harriet VanDerk, strolling into the form room.

CHAPTER 18

OK, so they *can* get worse. Maybe things can always get worse, and that's the life lesson here – *never* think things can't get any worse.

"Bog off, Harriet," says Natalie.

"Oh dear, oh *dear*," simpers Harriet gleefully.

"Are you deaf as well as ugly?" asks Amelia.

Harriet ignores them, preferring to give me a slow handclap instead. "*Brilliant!*" she proclaims. "Oh, how the mighty have fallen. I thought it was a bit suspicious that *you* might have had a good idea. But now we know – you hadn't. Nothing original has ever come out of your mouth, has it?"

"Just *leave*, you weirdo," says Nat, annoyed.

"It's fine," I say resignedly. This is now so awful

it's almost funny. *Almost.* "Let Harriet get it out of her system. I don't care."

"Oh, the irony," says Harriet. "Everyone's been acting like you're some kind of child prodigy, and you're actually a two-bit criminal."

"Yes, yes, very good," I say drily.

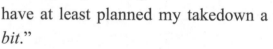

"So is *thief* going to be your legacy for the school yearbook, Jessica?"

"No, because I haven't stolen anything," I say tiredly. "Is that it? Not very witty, Harriet. I thought you might have at least planned my takedown a *bit.*"

"Harriet, if you don't get out of our form room *now*, you will regret it," says Natalie forcefully.

"Probably not as much as Jessica regrets getting caught," comments Harriet.

Natalie jumps down off her desk, and Harriet takes a step back.

"I didn't steal anything," I say flatly.

"Bit of a coincidence, though," says Harriet. "Surely? Or do you *really* expect us to believe that an insurance company copied an *eleven-year-old girl*?"

Natalie advances another step.

"I was going anyway!" Harriet waves a hand dismissively, then turns and stalks out of our form room.

"Thanks, Nat," I manage to say, but my head is buzzing with the implications of what Harriet just said.

"Any time, babes." Nat puts her arm around my shoulder and gives it a squeeze.

But all I can think is, *what if*? What if they *did*? As incredibly unlikely as it sounds, what if an insurance company *did* steal a dolphin cartoon from an eleven-year-old girl?

Am I *crazy*, I wonder as I ride the bus home. Have I actually lost my mind? I can't even tell. (Would you worry you were crazy if you were crazy?)

Tammy's always saying you can't trust mega-corporations because they have no morality and don't care who they squash to get ahead. But stealing a cartoon about dolphins?

"The paper called again," says Dad as I enter the kitchen.

"Really?" I ask tentatively. It's probably unrealistic to hope I will be getting my old job back.

"Yes, they're interested in your side of the story," he says.

"Oh, OK," I say.

"They said," Dad squints at a bit of paper in his hand, "they'll start with your apology, and then you could talk through the reasons you did it, and what you were thinking at the time."

"What?" I blurt. "I thought you meant I'd get a chance to defend myself."

"Doesn't look like it," says Dad. "They said they're particularly interested in any school or peer pressures that might have motivated you."

"But I *didn't* copy it," I say. My own words are starting to sound hollow and meaningless now.

"That's what I told them," says Dad. "I said Jessica

maintains she didn't copy anything and I for one believe her."

I feel a warm rush of gratitude towards my dad. "And what did they say?"

"They said they're only interested in an apology story, so you have to admit culpability or they won't print anything."

"Right, OK then," I say drily. Of course.

I start to feel angry. I've been so unjustly and shabbily treated! It's not *fair*.

Tammy joins us for dinner and I'm worried she will say my misfortune is karma for selling out and doing an evil advert. But actually she's really nice. Not only that, she's kind of *on the case*.

"OK," says Tammy, over Mum's minestrone soup. "I've looked into a few things. First, I've checked all the dates. The cartoon that I submitted to Newsworth predates any online versions by the insurance company by at least a week."

"Oh my God! This proves I didn't copy it, right?" I cry, excited. (Why has no one checked the dates before now? I suppose because it seemed so unlikely, but *still*.)

"Pretty much," says Tammy. "I took screen grabs

of everything too. It's amazing how quickly things can go missing when people start asking questions. Then I emailed the insurance company and asked them whether they'd like to explain themselves."

"Oh, blimey, OK," I say.

Tammy takes a slurp of soup and continues. "I'll give them twenty-four hours max to respond, then I'm taking the story to the activist online community. This is outrageous. An eleven-year-old is being bullied at school and losing her reputation, as well as paid work, because some adults wanted to make some money? It's a scandal."

I guess it is. Though part of me doesn't want to cause a fuss. Even though I'm angry. It's confusing.

?????

CHAPTER 19

OK, the dust has sort of settled a bit now. Tammy (amazingly) got to the truth. Apparently some new guy at an advertising company saw my dolphin cartoon online and didn't realise that anyone "owned" it. So he submitted it, along with a bunch of other ideas to their client, the insurance company, and it got picked.

The insurance company and the advertising agency are saying they had no idea where the cartoon came from and are blaming it all on the advertising guy. He says he didn't realise it would cause a problem, and that he didn't mean to cause trouble.

Tammy says she doesn't buy this story for a second, because even unscrupulous advertisers have codes of conduct and know what "intellectual property" is. She says they steal other creatives' ideas all the time, and get away with it by just changing things slightly.

She says this guy didn't even bother to change the cartoon but that the company probably thought they could get away with it because I'm eleven. (But apparently, legally this is just "conjecture" as Tammy can't actually prove anything.)

Tammy also thinks the guy is a coward, because when everyone noticed that the cartoons were the same, he should have come forward and admitted what he'd done, but he didn't. He let everyone think I was at fault, and let me take the rap for it. He claims he didn't know anyone was getting any grief because of what he did, but even *I'm* not sure if I completely believe that.

The "media" (our local paper and some bloggers) have all calmed down a bit now, and there've been a few articles about how ownership of ideas is a thorny issue in the digital age.

Tammy says it's amazing that everyone was so quick to judge me and give me a hard time, but the real culprit seems to be getting away with it.

Dad says that might be because the man has apologised loads and gone on record saying how awful he feels about it, whereas I never apologised. But then, I hadn't done anything!

Something good has come out of it, though. The insurance company were so embarrassed (and terrified of all the bad publicity) that they've offered to make a donation to the charity of my choice. I've chosen Green Fortis, the environmental charity where Dad works. This has also helped Tammy calm down, too.

GREEN FORTIS

It's *so great* being cleared and not in trouble any more. The relief is amazing.

The newspaper feels so bad that they just assumed I was guilty that they're bending over backwards to make amends. I've got my old job back and the editor-in-chief rang me to apologise *personally* and says they would like to run a story on "My World" so I can give my take on everything that's happened to me. I told them I'd think about it. I'm just not sure I need any more publicity right now.

"I mean, my hits are good, don't get me wrong," Mum is telling Tammy at our kitchen table over a cup of tea. "But they seem to have plateaued a bit."

I pour myself a glass of orange juice, managing not to trip over the dog, who appears out of nowhere halfway through this procedure.

"Well, that's good, though," says Tammy. "You'll probably find they stay the same for a bit, then go up again, then stay the same, then go up a bit. You're moving in the right direction."

"I know," says Mum. "Just part of me wishes I could get a little *push*, you know?"

"Of course," replies Tammy. "It's really difficult to get and then keep awareness high. That's what makes campaigning so difficult."

And suddenly I have an idea.

"Oh, wow! Look! There's my blog!" cries Mum as our family crowds round the local paper.

"This is great publicity for climate change," enthuses Tammy.

"Lovely mention of Green Fortis," agrees Dad.

"And Lady looks brilliant in her picture," says Ryan.

I decided to do the "My World" story for the local paper, on the condition that everyone I care about got

to plug their projects. So now "Jessica's World" is a whole page, full of pictures and promotional info. And all I had to do was agree it was horrible when everyone (except my family and friends) thought I was a liar.

So there's a mention of Mum's blog and how well it's doing; Tammy's climate-change charity (it was the least I could do, seeing as she cleared my name); more publicity for Green Fortis; a proper mention of my *Hell*fern comic, with pictures and how we launched at Comic-tacular; and finally a little mention of Ryan's "dog-training" and a picture of Lady from when we drew the Homer Simpson heads that time.

It feels really nice to use my "fame" for good, though I'm not sure it's all it's cracked up to be. It's really scary how quickly people can believe the worst of you. But helping other people has made me feel like I've taken back some control over the situation. And for once I don't mind being a springboard for everyone else. In fact, it's way more fun when it's collaborative, anyway.

Like I always say, I'm still totally grounded and down to earth. Maybe my legacy can be that I have given everyone *else* a leg-up, because *that's* how awesome I am. Haha, nah. My legacy is still my awesome cartooning.

CHAPTER 20

"I'm going to wear *some* black," says Natalie.

"Sure, but don't forget it's summer. You might be hot in black," replies Amelia.

"Yeah, but at night-time," says Natalie. "It will get cold eventually."

"But we'll be dancing – you'll still get hot," counters Amelia. "I'm not saying *don't* wear black. I'm just saying, *be aware* of black."

I'm sitting under the big beech tree with Natalie and Amelia, and they're discussing what to wear to the school disco. I think they might choose black.

I look down at the tree root I am sitting on, and wonder if it's the last time I'll ever sit on it. Nat and I have played around this beech tree the whole time we've been at Hillfern Juniors.

When it rains, muddy water collects in the gaps between the roots, and we used to pretend we were witches and they were our cauldrons. We'd get sticks and stir them, and pretend we were mixing potions for spells. We'd chuck in dead leaves, pretending they were magic ingredients.

I think I'll miss this tree, actually. I hadn't really felt that sad about leaving primary school, but now I get why some people have been a bit melancholy about it. I'm never going to make a potion in the beech-tree roots again. It's funny the things that bring home something is really happening.

"I have to tell you both something," says Amelia suddenly.

"Sounds serious," comments Nat. "Fire away." She smiles.

"I'm…" Amelia pauses. "I'm *not* going to Hillfern Seniors." (Natalie's smile slowly fades.) "My grandparents have offered to pay for my education, so I'm going to St Clement's Girls on the other side of town."

"When were you going to tell me?" cries Nat.

"Well, now," says Amelia. "We can still—"

"How long have you known?" interrupts Nat.

"Not long," says Amelia. (I'd wager she knew the day we got the key rings, though).

"I can't believe this!" Nat shakes her head despairingly.

"We can still hang out loads, like all the time. After school and at weekends," says Amelia.

"It won't be the same and you know it," says Nat.

"No, it won't be the same." Amelia looks at her sadly.

There was a time when this news would have been music to my ears. I'd have been delighted to be shot of Amelia and have Nat all to myself at secondary school. But I feel genuinely aggrieved, too. I finally just start liking the girl and she disappears? I feel *cheated*.

"I can't believe you're abandoning me," says Nat.

"At least you've still got Jess," says Amelia. "I'll be completely on my own at St Clement's. I won't know *anyone*. You'll know *loads* of people."

"So don't go. Come with *us*," says Nat.

Amelia sighs. "The thing is, I do actually *want* to go there. It's a really good school. It's the right place for me. I'm looking forward to making new friends. And you know, you will too."

Nat sighs. But she can't really argue with that. Part of me has been expecting her to storm off at some point, but instead she decides to be very grown up. "Well, then I'm happy for you. If that's what you want," she says stiffly.

But then she bursts into tears. So not *that* grown up, I guess. Amelia starts crying too, and they hug each other under the beech tree.

"Um, I'm not really in this," I say, extracting myself awkwardly. "I'll let you guys have a moment."

And I traipse back to the school, to my form room.

I don't look back at them. I want to remember the beech tree as the place where I was a witch mixing potions, not the place where Natalie and Amelia bawled their eyes out because everything was changing.

I hear Tanya's voice as I approach my form. "Here she is now," she's saying.

"Hi, guys," I say cautiously.

"Ta-da!" Tanya thrusts a piece of paper in my face. "Surprise!"

TA-DA !

"Thanks – what *is* this?" Flustered, I take the paper from her and hold it where I can see it.

"It's your *own* yearbook," says Tanya proudly.

Sure enough, I read the brightly coloured letters on the front, which proclaim "Jessica's Yearbook".

"We wanted to cheer you up when all that cartoon-stealing stuff was going on," explains Joshua. "And say thanks for promoting the comic in the paper."

"It's the story of us," elaborates Tanya.

"Told in comic form," adds Lewis.

"Open it," advises Joshua.

Inside is a comic strip about our lives.

"That's how we met." Tanya points to the first picture, which is of me and her in English. There's a speech bubble coming out of Tanya saying, "Oi, cartoon girl, draw *me* as a cartoon." Then the next picture is the *Tanya-as-a-Cadbury-Creme-Egg* that I drew.

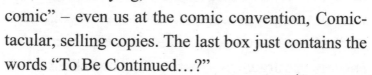

"This is amazing," I whisper. The comic strip goes all through our trials and tribulations: Tanya asking me to draw the school as hell, Joshua saying, "Let's make a comic" – even us at the comic convention, Comictacular, selling copies. The last box just contains the words "To Be Continued…?"

"Oh my God, this is the most amazing thing I have ever seen!" I laugh. "It's incredible!"

"So did we cheer you up?" asks Tanya, grinning.

"Yes! Thank you. This is awesome!" I'm genuinely touched.

This really seems like such a lot of effort to go to, just for me. It really makes me feel special and appreciated.

"I *knew* you'd like it," says Tanya, looking pleased with herself.

"Tanya got the idea for it sitting under the beech tree," says Joshua. "It just took us a little while to complete."

"It's my thinking spot," explains Tanya. Wow, that beech tree really is all things to all people.

"We've all got a copy of the comic strip too," says Joshua. "Something to remember everyone by."

"It's our *origin* story," explains Lewis.

"We felt we wanted to commemorate what we did here," adds Joshua. "I really enjoyed working on this with all you guys."

"It's been such brilliant fun," I agree. "You know, *between* the arguments and stuff." They chuckle.

"We're only human," says Tanya happily.

"That's why I put *To Be Continued* at the end," says Lewis. "I mean, we're all going to the same school next year."

"You in, Toons?" Tanya asks me.

TOONS

"Hell, yes!" I reply, without even pausing.

Tanya claps me on the back. "Good man, that woman," she says. Which doesn't make sense to me, but there you go.

It is at this point that Natalie and Amelia arrive at the form room, red-eyed from crying.

"What happened to *you*?" asks Tanya tactlessly. Then, eyeing Amelia suspiciously, "Was it you? I *knew* Toons forgave you a bit quickly. You're trouble, you are. Back on the bullying, are you?"

"No, no," I intervene quickly, remembering how little love there is between Tanya and Amelia. "Nat is sad because Amelia *isn't* going to the same school as us."

"Oh," says Tanya, seemingly confounded as she ingests this. Obviously she could only understand *delight* at that news. "Well, where's she going?"

Amelia sighs. "St Clement's."

"So Lady Muck is going to poshos school for posh people?" asks Tanya.

"Yeah, yeah," says Amelia.

"Well, each to their own," says Tanya reasonably. "No offence, but you might be better off with them, learning how to hold in your farts in Latin."

Natalie unexpectedly starts laughing, and then she can't stop. She doubles over hysterically, holding her stomach, and leans on a desk for support.

"Haha, you're … going … learn … hold farts in…" and then she's off into hysterical giggles again.

"I think you've cheered Natalie up," I tell Tanya.

"Good," says Tanya. "You've got nothing to be sad about, you weirdos," she tells them. Nat tries to reply but nothing comes out.

"Don't get people feeling sad about leaving primary school," says Tanya matter-of-factly. "That's like being sad you no longer wear nappies. I can't wait to get out there. The best is yet to come."

Tanya's wise words make me feel good about the future again. The weird nostalgia for the beech tree I was feeling is replaced by a simple happiness that I had the tree at all.

The tree will always be there in my past, and I will always have my memories. But I don't need it any more. That's not what it's for. It's for the next generation to play witches when it rains. I'm off, going places. It's the right time.

Plus, I know what I'm about now. Having been riding high and falling low with the fickle fame game, I just want to keep my head down and do the cartoon work without too much fuss, and build up a portfolio for my future.

I mean, I'm still really looking forward to secondary school and everything, and all it will bring. But what about my *career*? Exactly.

CHAPTER 21

"Hurry up, Jess, we're going to be late." Nat's parents are picking me up and dropping us at the end-of-term disco. Amelia is already in the car.

"It's cool to be late. We'll be fashionably late," I tell Nat as I put my shoes on and shout goodbye over my shoulder to my family.

The disco is in full swing when we get there. The dance floor is packed. Everyone is dancing to a Megan Flyer song. Then, as we head towards a table at the edge of the room with cups of squash on it, the DJ puts on a slow MBlaze number, and the dance floor empties amid groans.

Luckily the DJ learns from his mistake and doesn't do that again. He sticks with the more upbeat popular songs for a bit, and the dance floor gets busy again.

Natalie and Amelia want to play it cool to start with, so we go and drink our squash, surveying the scene. Harriet VanDerk comes over to get a drink.

"Oh, look who it is," says Amelia nastily. Oh, don't pick a fight with Harriet *now*, I think. We're supposed to be having a good time.

"Oh, hello," says Harriet disdainfully.

"I think you owe Jessica an apology," asserts Amelia. And don't use *me* in this game either, I think, annoyed.

"What for?" asks Harriet.

"You were very rude to Jess about her cartoon being stolen," says Nat. "And as you know, she's been cleared. You should say sorry for being so horrible."

Harriet puts down her cup of squash and looks at us, irritated. I think she's about to argue, but then she sighs. "Sorry, Jessica," she says quite earnestly.

"Oh, um, that's OK," I say awkwardly, surprised. "No worries at all." And with that, Harriet picks up her squash and heads off. *Phew*. That was actually relatively painless.

"Oh, by the way, Jess, while I remember," says Amelia. "Nat and I and some of the other members of D.A.F.T. had a vote on a new gang name the other day."

"*What?*" I say, alarmed.

"Yeah," says Amelia. "We've voted to rename it the Super Intelligent Cool Kids."

Wait… "*SICK?!*" I cry. "You want to rename the gang after vomit?" To my surprise they both burst out laughing.

"*PSYCH!*" hoots Natalie.

 "Haha! You totally believed us," says Amelia.

"I can't believe you believed us," says Natalie.

"I can't believe you said *psych*," I retort indignantly.

"We were actually considering Super Intelligent Chicks, though," says Amelia then.

"Because that would be S.I.C.," explains Nat. "The good kind. Then we got the idea to trick you and you totally fell for it!"

"Yes, yes, very good," I say politely. I can take

a joke. But really, with their track record with G.U.F. and everything, you can't blame me. Oh well. It's quite a good prank really.

We survey the scene a bit longer and then inevitably Natalie and Amelia want to dance. I cringe inwardly. I really don't feel like I'm a great dancer, but they grab my hands and soon we are messing about, jumping and bopping around on the dance floor, too. It's surprisingly fun.

Then the Megan Flyer song "Party Don't Stop" comes on, the song from the end of our school musical that Nat and Amelia made up a dance to, a dance we taught most of our year to perform.

Spontaneously, everyone finds their places and morphs into a synchronised group. There's a look in everyone's eyes that sort of says, "I can't believe we're doing this, but it's so naff it's fun."

We even still part like the sea, and let Tanya do her special witchy bit in the middle. I feel so happy that I was a part of how and why this happened. It's daft having one big legacy, I think, when really, we've all left a trail of lots of mini ones.

As the next song comes on, Joshua dances over to

us. He's doing his funny skids and clowning comedy, like when he was the Scarecrow, but still sort of dancing. His fringe is flopping in and out of his face.

"Care to dance?" He extends one arm. I gingerly take it, and suddenly he is whirling me around. It's like we're doing sort of very fast 1950s dancing with lots of swinging. (I don't know the names of any dances because I don't pay attention when my parents are watching *Strictly*.)

After a couple of songs I'm really thirsty, so we stop dancing and sit down by the squash table to get our breath back.

"You're a really good dancer," I tell him.

"Thanks, you're not so bad yourself."

"Ha*ha*," I say.

Emily, Megan and Fatimah come over to the table for some squash. "Hi, guys," says Emily. "Nice dancing."

"How funny was that when everyone did the Megan Flyer dance?" says Megan.

"Brilliant," agrees Fatimah.

"I hope we get to do stuff like that at secondary school," says Emily.

"I'm sure we will," I say.

"Yeah, it's going to be ace," says **ACE**
Emily. "We'll have to teach everyone the *would you rather* game, hey?"

"Definitely," I grin. I wonder if I'll end up in the same sets as the people I know. Be cool if we still got to shoot the breeze in art and play the *would you rather* game. They head off to find crisps.

"Hey," says Joshua. "I'm really glad we got to know each other." This seems a bit serious all of a sudden. I never know how to react when people are serious. That's partly why I make jokes.

"Me too," I say politely.

"Do you think things will be really different when we leave?"

"Hey, guys!" Cherry and Shantair come over to the squash table.

"So thirsty, so much dancing," says Shantair as they glug squash.

"Guess what, Jess, there is *definitely* a chess club at Hillfern Seniors," says Cherry. "Shall we join it?"

"Yeah, why not?" I reply. They head off again.

"I don't think they'll be *that* different," I say, smiling. "I mean, probably quite different in some ways, but you know, some things will probably remain constant."

"I consider you a good friend," says Joshua. "I hope that—" he begins, but I cut him off.

"Oh my God, they're *slow-dancing*!" I cry. "Nat and Amelia are slow-dancing with Daniel and Joe!"

A slower song has come on. Natalie and Joe are holding hands, standing a foot apart, stepping from side to side. Amelia and Daniel are actually sort of *hugging* and shuffling about. Both couples look slightly awkward. Natalie catches my eye and sees I'm laughing and scowls at me.

"Ah, leave them alone," says Joshua. "They can slow-dance if they like."

"Ha," I say. "They look funny."

"That's *very* mature," jokes Joshua.

"Oh, look who's lecturing *me* on being mature," I respond. I love joke-arguing with Joshua.

Instead of insulting me back, Joshua reaches out and takes my hand. I'm so surprised I go completely blank. Then Tanya arrives at the squash table and Joshua drops my hand again.

"'Ello 'ello," says Tanya. "Not a

bad party, not too shabby. Could do with more snacks, if you ask me."

"And the squash is too watered down." Amelia joins us.

"Where's your *dance partner*?" I tease her.

"Oh," she says, looking round. "I don't know. It's just a bit of fun. It's good practice to dance with boys, you know."

"I'll take your word for it," I say.

As the slow song ends, the lights come up and people groan.

"Oh my God. That's the end. That's the end of school," I say.

Tanya high-fives me. "Yeah, it is!" She beams.

A chant of "one more song" starts up from the direction of the dance floor.

"Do you want one more song?" asks the DJ.

"Yes!" shout the crowd.

"I can't hear you!" shouts back the DJ. **ONE**

"This DJ is an idiot," says Tanya. **MORE**

"I said, do you want one more song?" **SONG !**
he asks again.

"YES!" shout the crowd.

I'm about to defend the DJ to Tanya and say he's

not that bad, but at that moment he puts on the "The Grease Megamix".

Amelia facepalms. "*So* unoriginal," she mutters.

"Told you he's an idiot," says Tanya.

Nat starts shouting and gesturing for us to join her on the dance floor. Everyone's really going for it again.

I glance at Joshua. "Let's do it," he says.

The four of us link arms and head back to the dance floor. Then we all dance like crazy in spite of ourselves.

It really is a fun night. Some of the most fun I've had. *So far.* And it seems like a good send-off and way to say goodbye to school. I feel excited about what's going to happen next.

What has two thumbs and a bright future ahead of them? *This guy.* (I am pointing at myself with my thumbs, but making it look like a cool dance move.)

Acknowledgements

Massive thanks again to Suzy Jenvey, Kirsty Stansfield, Dom Kingston, Kate Wilson, Lindsey Fraser, Kathryn Ross and Sarah Horne.

I managed to finish the final draft of this book a few days before giving birth to my baby daughter, Phoebe, so I would also like to thank her for not coming too early and scuppering the plan. Good work, Phoebes. High five. (She leaves me hanging.)

And also thank YOU for reading.